Second Story

By Gus Gwynne

ISBN: 9781797437248

This is a work of fiction. Any resemblance to real persons, places,
events or groups is unintentional or is fictionalized and not meant to
comment on real people, events, places, or cultures.

This work contains some adult content of a sexual nature, and some
content of a violent nature, and may not be appropriate for minors
or all readers.

Author's Note: Names in novels can get confusing – especially
made-up names in Fantasy and Sci-Fi. I've tried to keep it simple
and fairly easy, but in case I missed on that, there is an appendix at
the end with some notes. The geography is inspired by Earth,
though the nations and cities are fictitious and not meant to refer to
any actual locations. Notes on the geography of the journey can
also be found in the appendices. The appendices do contain
spoilers, but might help if the names or places get confusing.

Table of Contents

Prologue

When the worlds were formed by the titans at the direction, will and whim of the gods, they were peopled with races made for the forms of their worlds. Many worlds were based on the element Earth, with Water and Air on the surface, for this pattern was fashionable with many of the gods. Most of these worlds were populated with varieties of humanity. The first humans, the nonborn, gave birth to all the generations that followed.

These worlds, each incomplete, came to be known as world-shards, or shards. Legend held that they were unfinished, and that the titans had rebelled against the gods and refused to finish them for reasons known only to those great and vast powers.

The might of the titans, the fuel of Creation, came from the Void – the vast emptiness between planets and stars, itself entirely antithetical to life, yet also the source of all worlds and all the infinite varieties of living things upon them. Those who lack the ability to control the Void can only survive in worlds and the simulacra of worlds, for the Void is too powerful and too raw for natural things to pass through it unscathed.

Many of the nonborn were inherently sensitive to the powerful forces used in their creation and could both sense and control the raw energy of Creation inherent in the Void. Later generations would call these energies of the Void "magic". Those awake to magic could pierce the vastness between worlds with their senses, seeing other worlds as clearly and detailed as the bulk of humans can see mountains on the horizon or islands in the sea. The least sensitive not only saw worlds as vastly far apart, but even had the edges of their worlds twisted so they appeared spherical. The most powerful saw different worlds as islands floating in the sky above and around them, like flying mountains, some almost close enough to touch.

Some of the weakest of those sensitives in the first generations learned to use magic to perfect themselves, making their bodies immortal, beautiful, graceful and strong. There were later named "elves". These were among the least sensitive, the least magical, but to mortals with no sense of the Void's power, they were marvels of perfection, and the subject of much envy or even worship.

A few of the most powerful took personal transformation much, much further. In their longing to visit the other worlds in the Void, which their eyes could see floating in the sky, a very, very few were able to channel enough of the Void's magic to truly transcend their bodies' limitations. Far beyond what the elves accomplished, these shed their humanity and took on the characteristics necessary to explore hostile worlds where Air was poison, or where Fire ruled the world instead of Earth. These were named "dragons". They were never numerous, but their legend spread to world after world as they explored the cosmos. Tales of them are found in every culture of every world they have visited, for they are awesome and beautiful, and also terrible in their fury and greed.

Fewer yet were those who grasped the reins of the Void itself, and took into themselves the power of Creation. These, who could twist the very laws of reality and change the fabric from which worlds were made, became the first wizards. Most could influence the shape of the world around them, conjuring elemental effects – jets of flame from thin air, tunnels carved in stone by the power of will alone, towers that defied gravity. Some few could even craft miniature worlds of their own in the Void – some to travel like dragons between worlds, others to isolate themselves from the worlds crafted by the titans.

Power and beauty draw envy. Great power inevitably crafts violent resentment.

Chapter 0: Before

In the most ancient of days, at the dawn of Creation, the most powerful of titans crafted shards of reality out of their own existence, manifesting the will and power of the gods from their own flesh to make Wish become Reality in the form of

> *countless worlds and fragments of worlds.*
> *These mighty spirits became the world-*
> *titans – their flesh the structure of lands*
> *and skies. It was needful unto the titans to*
> *have a means to speak across the limitless*
> *Void that they might know each other's*
> *efforts and successes. To this end were*
> *born the dragons – once human, but no*
> *more. – <u>Excerpted from "Tails of Creation",</u>*
> <u>*a history of dragonkind*</u>

Ariel stood on the highest point of the cliffs, looking down into the wide valley below. Newborn daylight glittered off of the river in the middle. The canyon walls of rough sandstone, glorious in shades of amber and gold and a thousand other hues in the morning light, descended in fits and starts, making innumerable spires, ledges, cliffs and rifts, from the high plateau where she stood to the valley bottom, nearly two miles below.

As always, she felt dwarfed by the landscapes away from Dragonhome. The whole spire of her birthplace could be lost in the immensity here. When she was younger, before she'd been allowed to travel far, she'd thought of Dragonhome as a huge place, but no longer. The last time she'd been there, it had somehow transformed into something small, cozy and comfortable.

Her father, whose truename she knew but kept secret even from herself, had brought her here to practice flying. She observed the valley below in *both* of the manners he had taught her.

First, with the senses of her young body and the calculations of her cunning mind. Second, and more important, with the magical vision only a dragon-soul can conjure.

Her eyes saw the jagged valley walls, and she knew the winds, a gentle breeze where she stood, would be like riptides near those. The river, so distant and pretty, would be a source of rising thermals later in the day, but would be a treacherous heat sink till it warmed up.

Air and water would fall and flow through the valley, coming from the high mountains and descending towards the sea.

The river flowed serene and placid below her. Men sailed boats on it, fishing or just enjoying the day. To a human standing in her place, it would have been a silver thread, barely a glimmer in the distance, but her dragon-eyes parsed the scene with easy clarity.

Air was far more capricious than water, of course. Heat and cross-currents made it a turbulent, treacherous stream, unsafe except in the middle of the wide valley.

Her chosen path was not in that calm middle. She had flown it many times when she was first learning her wings, but today was about a greater challenge.

Her sensitive ears heard the tale of the chaotic winds. Whistling, moaning, sighing and roaring from the highlands into the valley, it gave many clues to its secret patterns. Clues her father had taught her, that experience was slowly blossoming from "told" to "knows".

Taste and smell spoke mainly of highlands dust, with just the faintest trace of moisture from the river, but also of the plants and animals clinging to rough life on the cliffs and ledges below. Those were of little concern to her now, but she noted them in passing, as she'd been taught.

Touch was simple. The rocky ground she stood on atop the immense precipice, partially covered by thin, sandy soil, was solid under her four feet. The thin air and its currents against her skin spoke quiet volumes to her trained senses and powerful racial instincts, almost below her conscious threshold.

A human would call the early-morning uplands frigid. By noon, they'd be an oven of unbearable heat. She could see the temperature, and feel it as a sensation on her skin, but it couldn't harm her, so she paid it attention only insofar as it shaped the winds she would fly on.

But physical senses were not her only training – she was also learning the tricky excesses of dragonsight, though it had less to do with her eyes and more with her mind and spirit. The riptides, cross-currents, backflows and rapids of the air became things she could sense in her mind, even with her eyes closed. The stone beneath her, bright and colorful to ordinary vision, solid and unyielding to her touch, came to life as a darkness with the essence of endurance and strength, incarnate adherence to pattern, merciless in its lessons of impact and crushing. Elemental Earth, saying without words, "I hold up worlds".

Air, chaos incarnate, was forced into form by the earth where they met, though it took channel and direction unwillingly and was quick to kick and buck and twist back towards its habit of mayhem and disarray. Quickly, she was able to ken enough of the forced pattern that she could tell the best way to descend to the valley floor.

She rustled her wings, not yet unfolding them from her sides. She was ready.

Her father arched a knowing eyebrow at her. He knew she felt ready for the flight almost the very moment she made the decision. No words were spoken, nor were any needed.

He stood beside her in the shape he'd taught her was humanform. She still had trouble reading human faces, but her father's face she knew well enough to tell he was happy. Pleased, she thought, with how fast she'd traced out the flight path he wanted her to take.

One day, with enough experience, she would sense and know these things without having to take the time to parse them out consciously. But she was still learning. Only forty-three years old, still barely a toddler by dragon standards. Her father, nonborn and one of the first true dragons, had centuries of experience, and was an excellent teacher.

She was in her trueform. Though young, and still small compared to the immensity she would achieve at her full growth, she still made the full-grown man standing next to her seem slight. Her torso was the size of a large horse, with her graceful neck adding almost six feet ahead, and her serpentine tail stretching almost a dozen feet behind her. Her father and mother were large, even by draconic standards, and Ariel was bigger than most children of her age.

Other dragons, mostly mature males, told her she'd inherited her mother's good looks, and she hoped it was true. She knew that her glistening black scales and swirling golden eyes attracted more than a few glances her way when she was back home, and she liked the attention. Though she wasn't yet old enough to mate or even to desire to do so, it felt good to be called "pretty". The attention was nice, and she was vain enough to be flattered, while still young enough to be insecure about it.

Her mother, she knew, was considered beautiful, and was sought after by hundreds of drakes whenever she was ready to mate. Ariel didn't think her own gawky, spindly, young body could ever compare. That wasn't enough, however, to stop her from basking in the admiration and soaking up the flattery when she got it.

"Do you see the path?" her father asked. Though she knew humans considered his voice deep and impressive, she found all human voices squeaky and amusing. She'd never tell him that though. He would be mortified at the loss of dignity!

She nodded "yes" without speaking.

He replied, "I will wait for you here. Take your time. Fly safely. No tricks. Just fly to where I said, and come back. It will be quite exciting enough without diversion." He stepped aside as he finished, giving her room to extend her wings.

She stood up high on all fours, flexed the powerful flight muscles in her back and chest to extend her wings, and, as always before a new flight, wiggled her hips nervously. She heard a slight chuckle from her father ("We're not cats, you know?" she could almost hear him say for the thousandth time).

Her neck craned side-to-side as she took one last look. Her eyes swirled like metallic gold gone fluid as she extended her ken to scan the interface between earth's pure pattern and air's pure chaos one more time. She swallowed her slight nervousness and gave one last tiny quiver of anticipation, then sprang forward over the edge of the cliff.

Wind whipped her face and eyes!

Her wide wings caught the air and tamed it in an iron grip!

Steady and true, she flew with a grace uncommon for her age.

The strain on her flight-muscles was a glorious feeling, and her heart pounded in sheerest thrill as she supported herself mid-air.

The canyon walls flashed by and she had to resist the urge to swoop and frolic in the spires and cliffs. She was young, swift, and sure, but her father had told her to fly safely, so she did. Only a few flips and twirls, only a few dodges between stony spires, only a few hundred yards flying close enough to a cliff face that she could have touched it with her wingtip if she wanted!

And soon, too soon, she was at the bottom of the valley.

Her father had set her destination as a dwarven mining village where a tributary of the valley's main river came out of its own small side-canyon. Dozens of small men panned for gold in the stream or dug into the cliffs looking for the metal they were so expert at crafting.

She drew her wings in and plummeted towards the village, her face a dragon-smile as the dwarves scattered when she suddenly swooped over them! She snapped her wings smartly and stopped in mid-air mere feet above the ground in the middle of the village!

Tiny women and children, all bearded, all smiling, ran to gather round and admire the dragonling hovering in their town square. Children waved and cheered at her and she preened in the adulation.

And then it was time to fly back up. She gripped the air with her cupped wings and powerfully lofted herself back into the heights. Her mastery of the aerial domain was pure joy in her hard-working muscles and agile body.

By the time she got back to her father, she was soaring lazily on afternoon thermals. She circled gracefully high over his head, and then took an easy spiral down to where he was waiting patiently.

Her landing was simple and easy, raising only a slight puff of dust from the dry ground. Every move held a dancer's grace as the dainty, ton-and-a-half dragon touched down.

While she was away, her father had taken on his trueform. More than five times her length, and many times more than that of her mass, he was big even by dragon standards. His scales were a deep crimson, his swirling metallic eyes as black as deepest midnight, and he had golden highlights on his titanic wings and claws. Daughters often consider their fathers handsome, and Ariel was no exception.

Most important of all, he was smiling in pure draconic pleasure! She knew she had flown well, but seeing his smile and his approval made her warm all over and she ran to him and snuggled up to his side underneath his wing, rubbing her face on the base of his neck in joy. Her father, she was sure, was the best dragon in all the worlds!

***

Early on a morning that was full of mist and a drizzling rain, three riders arrived in the village. Their dark armor and black mounts ate the dim pre-dawn light and a hush came over the few villagers who were awake at that hour. Never before had lords of the Paladinate come to their unimportant village, and they were duly awed by the heavily armed and armored protectors who were sworn to defend the will of the gods in the kingdom.

They rode to the village's main hall, where the mayor lived. Dismounting, they did not tie their horses but left them saddled and ready to ride. The noble mounts were known for their courage, loyalty and strength, and none dared touch them for fear of the legends that they would kill any not a paladin who tried.

The mayor, hurriedly awakened and dressed, and the village elders, some still in their bedclothes, met the paladins on the porch of the hall. They greeted the lords with deep bows and deeper trepidation.

"Show us the child," the captain of the paladins told the elders as he strode past them and through the door into the meeting hall. Tall, even for lords of the Elder Blood, broad of shoulder, and with the scars of a hundred wars on his face, he intimidated by his very presence. The purity of his deep voice, and his nearly musical intonation, both common to his race, were lost on the awed and frightened villagers.

Like all people of that land, the captain of the paladins had skin and hair as dark as midnight, and eyes like polished mahogany. While most people wore their hair straight and shoulder-length, his was braided intricately in a dozen rows that ran back from his high forehead to the nape of his neck, where the braids joined into a larger braid that hung down his back nearly to his waist. The other two paladins, as befitted their lower, but still exalted, rank, had simple braids down to their shoulder-blades.

"Did someone call for them?" one villager whispered to another.

"Did the gods send them?"

"Are we truly cursed, then?"

So the mutters and whispers ran through the village, as person after person wondered one way or another about this strange visitation.

Quickly, the mother and father of the strange child arrived from their smithy on the far edge of town. His mother carried him in a blanket, wrapped up for warmth and comfort on the cold morning. Mist wetted their hair and clothing, and the father, Gerald the Blacksmith, was both uncomfortable and afraid. Amanda, the child's mother, however, stood proud and certain before the trio of warriors, and gently proclaimed, "Here is my child, Lord. He is perfect. I have named him Gem, because of his beautiful eyes."

The dour paladin lord looked into her unflinching eyes, and, though nobody else saw it, smiled briefly at her presumption and bravery. Then he took the child from her gently, holding him in both hands with the surety of one who had handled infants before.

Like all of the people of his parents' village, the baby had skin that was jet black, and hair that matched, but his sapphire-blue eyes were an anomaly that the elders and priests could not begin to explain. Nobody had ever seen eyes that color before in any human child.

There were whispers that his mother had slept with a demon, or that the child was cursed. Some, more optimistic, saw it as a sign from the gods that the long floods were finally going to end. The local priests had consulted auguries in their tiny temple, but to no avail. Something, some power, blocked their slight magic, causing no slight consternation on the part of both the temple and the villagers.

The three paladins gathered together. Their lord held the child, and the other two stood at his sides and each placed a hand on his shoulder. All three bowed their heads, and a gentle glow settled over them. Minutes went by without a sound or motion, as if all four, paladins and child, had become light-filled, lifelike statues.

Long that vigil seemed to all the people gathered there. Never had they seen true magic before, and they were fearful of it, though they knew the paladins were sworn to defend them and could do no evil deed.

After minutes that seemed hours, the glow faded, and the paladin lord handed the child back to his mother gently, this time smiling so that all could see it. "We find no taint in this child", he calmly announced. His voice was quiet, but everyone gathered there heard him clearly. "His full destiny is hidden from us by some power, but it is not an evil power. He will walk a dark path, of that we can be sure, but what darkness and towards what destination we cannot see. Whatever path it is, the gods have neither blessed nor cursed it, and he and his family are to be accorded no special honor nor fear because of it."

With that, the paladins strode purposefully from the hall and remounted their warhorses. In minutes, they had disappeared into the mist and fog as quietly and suddenly as they had appeared, leaving behind years of gossip and wondering.

Chapter 1: Noble Plans

*When the nonborn were no more,
but memories of them still held fresh, the
Lady Magistrix of Xalax was challenged by
the Death Horde of Trialak for supremacy
over the world and wizardry within it.
Battle was joined betwixt the two, and,
though her enemy was numberless as the
blades of grass in a field, and boundless as
the very sea, the Lady triumphed. All the
peoples of the many lands of the world
united in their approbation of her, and
pledged their undying devotion. First and
most powerful of wizards, wise with
centuries of experience, beautiful as
Nature itself, and gifted with cunning and
dauntless courage, she ruled the world,
and all rejoiced in her beneficence. – From
the official histories of Xalax*

The room was filled with expensive furniture, rare books, gilded fittings, colorful art, and people who matched or outshone the ostentatious decor. The whole was well-lit by expensive, scented candles in expensive, polished lamps, hung from expensive, well-crafted fittings, on expensive, heavily decorated walls and stands. Only a dragon's lair could possibly have been more lavish.

A dozen lords and ladies had gathered to discuss the future of the city they effectively owned, along with servants and slaves for each, secretaries and assistants and numerous armed guards. Their muted voices, speaking soft pleasantries to one another and crisp demands to their servants, but never directly addressing their slaves (too gauche), filled the room with a soft murmuration.

There was a faint knock at the door, followed immediately by the entry of the final member of their council. The Lady Urula, clothed as usual in an exquisite dress, this time a creation of black and white silk, with gold, ivory, and a swath of tiny gemstones stitched to it, had finally arrived, and they could now address the business that had brought together all of the most powerful people in the city.

Lord Geor, with the body of an adult man in his second decade, had the mind of an infant. Everyone in the room knew he was there merely to grace the meeting with his lofty presence, but that his lowborn wife, Lady Audep, would be the one who wielded the considerable power and wealth that was legally his but had been factually hers since they were married at the age of six.

Lady Urula, second in prestige only to Lord Geor, was quite the opposite. Already in her early twenties, she was unmarried (though beautiful and rumored to have a wide taste in disposable lovers), over-educated, and brilliant. She had inherited a title and vast debts when her lord father had died, and had since built her once-depleted family fortune from the brink of bankruptcy to heights that were rumored to be beyond even that of the banking and merchant guilds.

As the traditions of their people demanded, she could only marry a common man, not a noble, and many had tried to catch her fancy, but she was rumored to dally and then spurn. Suitors had grown rare in recent years as most gave up hope of sharing her vast fortune.

The least prestigious noble in the conference was the elderly Lord Vurn, who was almost eighty years old. His current wife, the sixth to bear that title, was barely past puberty. She couldn't attend the meeting, since she was pregnant – the child would officially be his twentieth, but was in reality the first-born of Vurn's captain-of-the-guard. Only two of Lord Vurn's heirs were actually related to him in any way, and one of those only because he was actually the son of Vurn's younger brother. The lord was very proud of how many children he had spawned on all of his young wives, and was the only person in the city who didn't know that only one of them might actually be his, and even that one was somewhat doubtful.

While he was the least influential noble in the room, he commanded vast fortunes, owned huge swaths of the city's land and the farms around it, and had a small army of loyal armsmen. His power was real and substantial. He was only "least" because the others had even greater dominion and wealth than he, not because he lacked authority of his own.

Not in a handful of decades had so much power and wealth gathered in that city in a single meeting. It was a dire time, and they were the ones with the most to lose and the most ability to do something about the threat to their rule.

Lady Xath, yet another power of the city, who used expensive fashions and jewelry to make up for a face that only a greedy flatterer would call attractive, called the meeting to order as soon as appropriate greetings had been made to and by Lady Urula.

"My peers, we are gathered this day to discuss a grievous situation. Our city is threatened by the vast armies of Tri-Lek, and we will soon be conquered by those barbarous hordes unless we, those of us in this room, do something to stop them. We all agree, do we not, that we haven't the manpower to defend ourselves successfully when they attack us? Is it thus, or does any of you have a plan for martial success?"

Lady Urula made the slightest motion with her head, and Lady Xath recognized her wish to speak.

Lady Urula addressed them. "I have word of a mercenary army which is reputed to wring success out of impossible odds. They are expensive, but their reputation is quite fearsome."

When she mentioned "expensive", several of the nobles flinched. If she considered them expensive, with her unlimited wealth, then the price must be stratospheric indeed.

She continued. "I do not suggest we give up other avenues of recourse. If we can divert the hordes away from us, perhaps against one of our rivals to the east, that might be best. However, if such diversions do not succeed, perhaps these blades-for-hire could help as a failsafe."

Lord Bism, who was considered to be of moderate means by this group, spoke the question many were afraid to ask. "Lady, I hate to be so uncouth as to haggle over a price that has even been named, but how 'expensive' are they? If you indeed know? And how are we to apportion their costs if we do effect this plan of yours?"

The lady replied, "I will pay all of their costs myself. After all, I live in this city that we wish to defend. It is my plan, and I will finance it myself."

Most present thought she was making the first foolish decision of her life. A few simply felt relief that they wouldn't have to pay to save their own hides. Of all present, only Lord Geor's world-wise wife questioned what the price of that generosity would end up being, and even she kept her doubts to herself.

Weeks passed and city after city to the south was reduced to smoking rubble by the ever-closer barbarian horde. Hundreds of thousands of people were slain in battle or slaughtered helplessly, thousands more forced into slavery. Even the noble-born weren't spared, and stories were common of rape, slavery, even death, for whole families that had ruled wealthy cities for generations. Dozens of cities that had stood since the days when the world was still being made were razed to the ground. And still the horde came on, its thirst for bloodshed, loot and conquest unquenchable.

The people of the city spent their days in fear and uncertainty. The nobles worked through plan after plan, stratagem after stratagem – only to see each fail in turn. The day they got word that the mercenaries were on their way and were willing to accept the contract was the same day their scouts reported the horde had entered the mountain passes to the south and was on its way to them with no chance of being diverted.

Chapter 2: Mercenaries

"Let there be no mention of he who leads the rebels against me," proclaimed the Lady Magistrix. "His existence is

purged. His records are dust. None may challenge me and live!"

For the Lady had been betrayed. A nameless traitor, pretender to her throne, from which she ruled in right of wisdom, power, majesty and justice. A betrayer who, foolish with lust for power, thought he could challenge the Lady herself, the most powerful wizard in all the worlds.

A liar, who spread false tales about the Lady and the Horde of Trialak. Despite all witness and record to the contrary, the traitor claimed that credit for victory lay not with the Lady.

But history has shown that traitors never prosper. Liars are caught in the very webs of deceit they weave. And those who challenge the Lady do not live to brag nor benefit of it. – from the official histories of Xalax

Gem barely looked at the city as he rode towards it. Years before, when he'd first left his home, he'd been awestruck by the first real city he saw. His home village had only a couple of dozen families in it, and a few dozen more spread out on farms around it. His first city had been a shock to him, with hundreds of people jammed into what had seemed a dense crowd at the time. Since then, he'd seen cities with hundreds of thousands of people jammed together till the smell alone was enough to drive tears from his eyes. Cities weren't interesting anymore.

This particular city's name was "Xalax", and he knew little more of it than that. He assumed, correctly, that it had been named after one of its nonborn founders in the Days of Creation.

It was built of a mix of wooden, adobe, and brick structures, with no planning, no sense of order, and not a straight street in it. There were several tall mansions at the foot of the high cliff that backed the city, and that was as close to a definite neighborhood as it had. The rest was laid out haphazardly with no plan, no logic, and no sense of a need for such.

His companions, eight tough men, were too busy telling lies, jokes, stories and gossip to each other to pay much attention to Xalax either. They were all caked in weeks of road-dust and the remains of their own sweat, and they and their horses all looked more than a little ragged. Any seeing them would have been forgiven for assuming they were dangerous paupers without a penny between them. Even so, they'd left a few bandits drowning in their own blood over the miles – desperate people don't pay much attention to appearances.

Gem knew the cause of the desperation in this land. Lands to the south had been gutted by an army out of the deep southlands, and refugees were homeless, hopeless, and inclined towards either cowardice or violence by the shocks they'd been through. The loss of trade and the fear and uncertainty were spreading the desperation far beyond the lands the barbarians had pillaged, and many people had lost more than they knew they'd ever had.

The land Gem and his men travelled through was lush, full of rich farms, thriving forests, vast herds of both tamed and untamed beasts. Unchecked, the horde of Tri-lek would reduce it all to burned ruin and death.

It was the hot season, so the clay-packed roads were dry and dusty, putting up a fine silt that stuck to skin, irritated dried noses and eyes, and tainted everything that went into the mouth till life tasted like dirt – but even in this weather the land prospered. Life here was made for this kind of summer, and for the wet, cold winters that followed it.

The giant mountains to the south, the highest Gem had ever seen in all his travels, sent numerous rivers running through these lands, while also blocking the seasonal monsoons that deluged the lands south of them. Every year, the irrigation systems built from those rivers kept more and more land bountiful even in the hottest parts of the year. The endless rivers also fed the numerous complex aqueducts of Xalax and all its surrounding towns and villages.

Gem had never travelled here before. War was almost unheard of in these vast lands. Too few people in too much land made for small reason to fight, and too much distance to fight over. His wealth, such as it was, had been made to the east, in lands more densely populated and more lucrative and easier to fight over.

When he did look at the city he was coming to, he saw a sprawling place. Not tightly packed like the bigger cities to the east, or the giant cities on the other side of the eastern ocean. Xalax didn't really have definite border – it just gradually spread out, with buildings getting further and further apart till they couldn't rightly be called "neighboring" any more. There was no demarcation between the city itself and the surrounding farms and ranches.

But he could see where they had started building a rough palisade around part of it. It was desperate and futile, and wouldn't stand against their invaders for more than a few minutes, if even that. But it at least meant they were trying, however impotently, to defend themselves.

Not that it would matter. The outcome of the war was inevitable and nothing the people of the city did now could change how it would turn out. The end was as inevitable as the tide, as foredoomed as the seasons.

In the late afternoon, Gem and his men arrived at a crudely built, and obviously new, gate in the half-built palisade, and were met by a dozen armed boys. Not one had seen his twentieth summer, and Gem knew none had seen any fight more serious than a bar brawl. They wore ragtag bits of armor and carried makeshift weapons, and their every move and thought showed they had no experience with either item.

In an over-loud, officious tone, the biggest of the boys challenged Gem. "Turn away, you men. We're not taking refugees into our city right now."

One of the others, half-hiding behind his larger cohort, piped in with, "Especially brigands. We never want your type in here."

A couple of the boys laughed that nervous semi-giggle that means a man is trying to convince himself that he's brave. A few others swallowed and just got goggly-eyed at Gem and his company.

Andwer, one of Gem's companions, rode forward till he was almost up with his captain. In a deep, friendly voice, a voice a kindly father might use to address an unruly but loved child, he told the "guards", "You want to let the captain and us men pass. We're wanted in your city." He held up a piece of paper that had words on it like "safe passage," and "Lady Urula".

Gem heard Saluem, behind him, muttering, "Or we could just ride straight through this sorry lot and let them sort it out with their superiors if they live through it."

The leader of the guards was still trying to read the piece of paper. It had far too many long words on it, like "consequently" and "obligation", that, even had he been able to competently sound them out, he would have been no wiser as to their meaning, so it was taking him longer than Gem had patience for.

Gem spoke up. "Lieutenant," he addressed the young man. "You *will* let us into the city. One of your men will guide us to a suitable inn, where we may clean up and dine before your man takes me to confer with Lady Urula. We need suitable accommodations, and we need them now." His speech had the precision of intonation and grammar that scholars affected, without the slightest hint of any accent.

He continued while the whole guard contingent stared at him in shocked disbelief. "You will either do this because you have your own best interests at heart, or you will do this because we make you do this, or you will do this because the Lady will pay you to do it. One way or another, you will do this."

The leader of the guards, named Telso, looked for the briefest moment as if he were about to disagree. Then suddenly, to the shock of all of his men, who knew him as a prideful bully, he bowed and capitulated completely.

"Casu," he addressed one of the young guards, "take them to the Red Rooster, and see to their needs." With a sweep of his arms, he gestured for the rest of his men to clear the way for Gem's company.

Casu had recently finished his fourteenth year of life, was of middling height for his age, and had the build and look of the street-tough that he aspired to become. Like many of the natives of the region, he had dark brown skin, black hair, light hazel eyes, and the scars on his face matched the scars on other young men's knuckles, as their facial scars matched his worn hands. His manner was beyond nervousness and fully into panic-anxiety, and it showed in his eyes, his fluttering hands, and his stiff shoulders and neck. It was already hot out, so his fear-perspiration was somewhat hidden.

Casu hurried to Gem's horse and bowed briefly. He didn't know what was going on, and it frightened him. There was a horde approaching Xalax from the south – already on its way through the mountain passes if the rumors were to be believed – and now he had strange men doing strange things at the gate he'd been recruited to guard. The men were heavily armed and had the look of bandits or raiders, and somehow their odd-looking leader had cowed Lieutenant Telso merely by looking at him.

If Casu had been a career armsman, a real soldier or guard of some sort, he would still have been worried about the horde and about Gem and his men. But he was a career loiterer who'd been swept up by the nobles' efforts to create the first army in Xalax's history, and he was in a constant state of near-panic. Mere "worry", much less "professional concern" – even these would have been a monumental *improvement* in his mood.

He and his friends were accustomed to spending their days dicing, drinking, bullying merchants, and fantasizing about more expensive prostitutes than their meagre income of shakedown money allowed. Now, as official city guards, they spent their days dicing, drinking, bullying travelers who wanted into the city, and fantasizing about any women who walked into view, while being paid to do all that – so long as they did it at the city gate and wore ribbons on their arms that said they were official and had ranks.

It was a new sort of life for him, and he wasn't used to it yet despite being on the job for almost two weeks.

So he had no idea how to deal with Gem's demand of guidance to an inn. He thought about asking to ride behind one of the men. He thought about sending for a mount (and briefly wondered how he'd go about doing that, if it was even something he was allowed to do). He settled for walking next to Gem's horse's head since that seemed to involve the least risk.

He also decided that anyone who could intimidate Telso that easily was worth a bit of respect, if not outright terror, so he addressed Gem cautiously. "My lord, if you'll please come with me." His voice only broke twice.

After that brief statement, Casu kept quiet while he guided them. He was too afraid to make small-talk of any sort, and none of them asked him any questions.

Gem's men were of sorts he'd seen before. Xalax's population was brown-skinned, with straight black hair and dark or light brown eyes. Men from the east had paler skin with the cast of ochre, and their faces had a different shape around the eyes and cheeks – he'd seen many of those in his life. Men from across the eastern ocean had similar features but their skin tended towards coppery shades. Men from the south and the far west had darker brown skin and curly black hair. A few of the barbarian races of the far north-west had pale skin and light eyes.

Since Xalax was positioned as a major way-station on the far-reaching east-west trade routes of the world, Casu had seen people from all of those lands throughout his life.

Gem's men had those looks. One had strange reddish hair and brown dots all over his face, above a wild-man's snarl of unkempt beard, and the skin of the northern barbarians. Another had skin of darkest brown and the features of the farthest south. And the rest had normal eastern or far-eastern looks.

They were uniformly big men, with tough faces and hard eyes and the heavy muscles of blacksmiths – Casu had never seen professional soldiers before, but he was familiar with the nobles' guardsmen and these had that sort of air to them, taken to an extreme.

Their leader, however, was the strangest man Casu had ever seen. His skin was the pure black of a coal cellar at midnight, and his eyes were an impossible shade of glittering pale blue. Unlike his men, he kept his jet-black hair short, and his face and hair were impossibly clean despite the omnipresent clay-dust from the road. The dust coated his clothing, armor, and horse, but somehow left his skin, hair, and even his sword, clean.

Casu kept glancing at the sword – he'd never seen one before – and at Gem's plate-steel armor. He also couldn't keep from staring at Gem's strange face. He wasn't cut in the forms Casu was used to, with features unlike those of any land he'd ever seen before. Gem's hair was shorn so short it stood up from his head a finger's thickness, and his cheeks and chin had the hairless smoothness of a youth he had obviously long since left behind. His age was hard to judge, perhaps he was in his third decade? The few scars he carried from his many battles added to a look that was hard beyond whatever years he did have.

It was also strange to Casu that the leader – called "Captain" by his man back at the gate – was by far the smallest of the men in the band. With all of them up on horseback, Casu couldn't really gauge height, but he could easily tell that Gem was much smaller than any of the others. Casu was used to the biggest man being the undisputed leader of any group.

It took a few minutes to ride to the Red Rooster. When they arrived, Gem dismounted and told Casu and his men to see to the horses while he made sure the place would suit them.

Gem strode into the common room of the inn, slapping his gloves on his legs in a small cloud of gray dust. He'd been on horseback on the road since before the sun came up, and the day was both old and overly hot, so he was looking forward to a cold drink and food that hadn't come out of his saddlebags.

He was, by local standards, on the short side, at no more than 5'6" tall, but broad shoulders and a heavy chest over a flat stomach well-hinted at strength that was beyond his size. Women often found his grace and poise attractive, even those who weren't fascinated by his foreign features, black skin, and strangely colored eyes.

As he came in, some of the patrons stared openly at his alien appearance, but most prudently looked away quickly when he caught their eyes.

The innkeeper, named Kon, greeted Gem respectfully, in a deliberately neutral tone, without the warmth he gave the local regular customers, but without the hostility he saved for the street gangs. "Welcome, sir. How may I help you," he asked casually.

Gem looked around. The place looked clean and respectable enough, without being too high-class for his crew.

He walked to the bar and replied, "Right now, my men and I need to wash some dust out of our throats. Something cool to eat would go well with a bit of ale. Have you any fresh fruit, or salad that hasn't been sitting in the heat all day?"

Kon looked at the ragged, dust-covered figure Gem presented, and wondered about coin. He also looked at the rough face, the steel-hard eyes, and the heavy weaponry, and decided to ask later. Without a word, he scooped a mug of cold ale out of a barrel behind the bar, and let his face ask the question of how many more were needed.

Gem held up eight fingers and then took a seat at one of the crude wooden long-tables near a window and away from the hearth.

Kon sent one of his young sons to the nearest market to get some fresh fruit or salad – he stocked no such thing, but decided that quickly obtaining some was the wisest choice.

Gem waited till the innkeep had sent a boy off on the errand, then caught his attention. When Kon looked his way, Gem flipped a flashing coin through the air to him. Kon caught it, and was about to lament simple copper or brass when he realized what he was really holding. He'd never even seen a gold coin before! He'd hoped for a small silver, and instead he had a gigantic disk of solid gold in his hand. He stared at the coin, bit it to test if it was real, and then stared wide-eyed at Gem.

After that, Kon was all solicitous service and fawning attention. That coin, by itself, was more than the whole inn usually made in a week. It was enough to buy a small farmcroft or a healthy horse, and this strange man tossed it around like it was copper!

When Casu led Gem's men into the inn a few minutes later, Kon glared at them till he realized they were with Gem, and then his hostility switched to affability and wide smiles.

Casu, who knew nothing of the gold coin, was perplexed. Kon was no fool, and he wouldn't own an inn if it didn't get along with strangers, but he had a horde of smelly, filthy, dangerous giants in his common room, and he was acting like they were noble-lords on a charity-walk.

Casu's errand was complete. The captain and his men were at the Red Rooster. That was all Telso had told him to do, and he assumed he was supposed to get back to the gate now. But the captain gestured for him to approach.

"You know this town, right lad?" he asked.

Casu nodded affirmation. "Yes, sir. Been here my whole life."

Gem smiled. "How would you like to earn a bit? I'll need a guide to Lady Urula's home once I've cleaned up, and we'll need a local guide and ambassador for the duration of our stay."

Casu wasn't sure how that fit with his duties as a city guard, nor what "ambledsor" meant, but he liked the sound of extra income, and he was scared to tell Gem "no", so he smiled and replied, "I can help you, sir," in a voice filled with a mix of solicitude, fear and respect.

Gem nodded. "I thought you might be able to! Glad to have you with us." He looked up at Kon and gestured for one more drink and pointed at Casu. Kon understood and sent over another mug.

Once they'd eaten and drunk their fill, Gem told Kon to arrange for clean sauna-baths. "Make sure the rooms don't stink, the water is fresh from a clean rain-barrel – nothing from a horse-trough or that sewer you call a river. And some healthy girls to help us get clean. Plenty of heat and no smoke."

Kon was happy to tell him that he had clean saunas on-premises, and that he could certainly send for the right kind of girls. "Do you want anything in particular? There are specialist houses around, and they'll send over whatever you want for the right coins."

"No children, no crones, and no itch in the groin. Other than that, whatever you have will suit my men just fine."

The men overheard the conversation and Kethen chimed in, "And no goats, despite what Andwer may beg from you."

Saluem teased Casu. "Watch out for Andwer, lad. He's likely to stick himself in any hole he can catch, and he might rip a little guy like you in half!"

Andwer barked, "Hey, the goat was just that one time!"

Kethen ribbed him, "And the mare was supposed to be only one time, but she kept coming back for more." He turned to Casu, "Darn animal said that stallions just weren't adequate after what Andwer did for her!"

All eight laughed.

The banter kept up as they followed Kon to his saunas. When they got there, Casu realized he was afraid to go in with them. Gem pulled him aside and quietly calmed him. "Don't worry. They joke a lot, but you can trust them. I wouldn't keep a rapist in my troop. You're safe."

Casu felt like he should have been shocked at the suggestion that he might be raped by the men, but a calmness spread through his mind and he decided it didn't really matter. He was safe, and they were just joking around like men do.

Now that he was standing next to Gem, Casu realized that the captain was at least an inch or two shorter than Casu himself was. He was looking down into the captain's face. That should have made him feel bigger and more powerful than the soldier, but it didn't. Despite his lack of height, Gem gave an impression, almost an aura, of being fully in command of everyone and everything around him.

Filthy clothing was quickly stripped off, and then they all trooped into the baking-hot sauna. Steam began to filter the smell of road-filthy men out of the air. Kon's employees brought buckets of warm water, and everyone doused thoroughly.

Again, Casu was struck by Gem's odd appearance. The rest of the men had body-hair normal to their type – most had the curly chest-hair normal to adult men, and all had varying amounts of hair in armpits and groin. Except the captain, who was hairless below the neck.

Casu was glad he'd been warned about Andwer. Otherwise, he might have stared in shock. The big redhead's manhood was at least thrice the size of anyone else's.

Everyone was relaxing in the heat when a dozen women were ushered in by Kon. Casu blushed and stared – he'd never been able to afford women like these! It was like being surrounded by naked goddesses!

At first, they all took turns either admiring Andwer or pretending to be afraid of him, but then they spread out among the various men and started helping them to scrub and bathe.

They were all ages and looks. One was barely old enough to have hair between her legs and breasts like bumps on her chest. Another had a patch of gray in her hair and the heavy breasts that age and motherhood provide.

Gem sent the near-child away. "Too young for this rough crowd," he told Kon. He paid the girl anyway, a generous pair of the middle-sized silver coins known as "merchants" in that land. When Casu asked why he paid without services, Gem explained, "So she can eat tomorrow without being punished by her pimp tonight."

Casu was confused. He'd never considered that anyone could care whether another was punished or not. Gem answered his unasked question, "I can't save her from her life. Only she can do that. But I can at least make sure I'm not the cause of suffering for her. If I sent her away empty handed, she'd be punished for failing. Through no fault of her own, I refuse to allow anyone in my employ to violate certain rules. We protect children like her, we don't use them."

Casu had to think about that. He'd lived his life on the streets, and it was every man for himself. Rules were what you got punished for breaking, if you got caught by someone stronger than you. The idea that someone might have rules about protecting other people was alien to him. It took him a moment to realize that the captain was telling him that he, Casu, was also being protected by the captain's rules.

That was clear enough to him, but it made him both more comfortable and less. More because he was safe and knew it, for the first time in his life. Less because it was making him think in new ways.

Gem cleaned up quickly, and then indicated Casu and he would be leaving to go see Lady Urula. Some of the women giggled and smiled and tried to convince him that staying would be more fun, but he insisted on leaving anyway. "More fun for the rest of them," he said with a big grin, sweepingly indicating his eight men.

Casu didn't want to keep the captain waiting, and he definitely didn't want to keep the city's most wealthy and important noblewoman waiting, so he dressed fast.

Lady Urula owned the streets and buildings Casu lived in and around, and was powerful enough to collect protection money from every resident and merchant in the whole area of the city. Casu wasn't curious about meeting her, he was intimidated to his deepest core!

Gem paid a handful of copper coins to one of the inn's slaves and asked him to clean up his men's armor and clothing for him. "Dust and polish the armor, but don't touch the weapons, please." Casu was, again, surprised that the captain would pay a slave for what could be had free, and that he would use a word like "please" with one.

Theoretically, a slave could buy itself and then grant itself freedom, if it earned enough money. But in practice it almost never happened because nobody paid them, and a slave caught stealing would be put to death, so they never had enough money to buy themselves. Free men would get a hand cut off for theft, but slave punishments were always much more harsh.

Again, Gem seemed to know what Casu was thinking without asking. "Just because he was born as property doesn't make him any less than human. People need to be free. We're not healthy if we aren't. I can't free him – people can only do that for themselves, truly – but I can at least give him the idea."

Casu was beginning to realize that the captain's odd appearance was perhaps the least unusual thing about him.

Casu only had his own clothing, so he put it back on despite it being dirty. Gem dressed in plain cotton, a simple tunic and pants, and some clean sandals instead of his riding boots. It was peasant-garb, but Gem had an air that made him both noble and dangerous. Regardless of how he dressed, no one would ever mistake him for a farmer or craftsman.

Instead of taking his own, very tired, horse, Gem paid for a rickshaw taxi to take them to the lady's home.

Casu was expecting Gem to overpay, but he paid the taxi-man exactly what he had been asked for. "A free man doing the service he's chosen. He gets paid the right amount and would be insulted if I patronized him with a large tip or overpay."

It didn't even occur to Casu to question how Gem had known his question, or the taxi-man's opinions on pay and pride. It was the strangest day ever, and he was beyond questions by this time.

Neither Casu nor the taxi-man had been to the noble section of town before, but between them they figured out a route that eventually got them there. A few questions to street-guards got them to the lady's large estate at the base of the cliff that overlooked the city. Gem paid the taxi-man to wait, and convinced the gate-servants to give him a place to rest and a meal and drink while he waited.

Casu belatedly realized how underdressed he was for a noblewoman's house and begged to be left with the taxi-man and servants. Gem didn't mind and let him stay at the gate. One of the household servants took Gem to the giant foyer of the main house and asked one of the butlers to take a message to the lady that she had a guest.

The request was essentially, "There's a poor person here who claims to have business with our lady. He's probably lying, but you never know, so please ask her. He says his name is 'Gem', and he looks very strange and might be dangerous."

The household guards left two men watching Gem as he waited. They wanted to keep him standing, out of respect for the house and lady, but when he seated himself on one of the benches on the front porch, neither could bring himself to object.

Gem stood when the lady and her bodyguards arrived. As appropriate, her personal guards were armed women – they wore studded leather and were armed with daggers and short spears, and carried themselves like they knew how to use both.

Lady Urula herself wore a dress of expensive foreign silk, and a small fortune in jewelry, but was much less formally and expensively dressed than she had been at the noble meeting all those many nights ago. She was wearing a fortune that would purchase a small estate in the country, but she didn't think of it that way. It was one of her comfortable-about-the-house outfits and she thought it quite informal.

She was beautiful, and knew it. Her dark brown skin and shiny black hair were offset by the bright colors of the cloth draped over her. She had brown eyes that glittered with life and intelligence, set in a face with delicate features that many men found irresistible. Her body was young, and had the grace of a dancer and the subtle curves that go with a slender build. In place of the usual floral perfumes favored in her land, she scented herself with sandalwood and incense in the sauna – more subtle and exotic than her peers.

Instead of having her servants or guards speak for her, she addressed Gem herself. "Are you the mercenary captain known as 'Gem'?" she asked in a musical voice.

Gem bowed his head slightly. "I am," he replied simply. His dark, deep voice sounded rough compared to hers.

The lady bowed her head the exact same amount as he had, as though he were her equal. "Then we have business to discuss, Captain."

She led him to one of her sitting-rooms and had crystalline glasses of iced fruit juice served, then shooed her guards and servants away. She did not offer food, since that would put obligations on her that she wasn't sure were appropriate yet.

Once they were comfortably settled, she got straight to the point. "Captain, let me be blunt. My city is under a threat that we cannot survive on our own. I have heard your reputation, and the … rumors or myths … that say your victories are not the simple result of martial prowess and strong men. My peers would dismiss such out of hand." She paused a moment to see if he reacted to this, but his face did not stray in the slightest from an expression of polite attention and conservative interest.

After a moment, she continued. "I do not know the truth of these rumors, but I believe in the possibility of them. So I will simply ask, are you capable of the things they say you can do? Can you and your handful of men win this battle and somehow save my city?"

Gem hadn't expected anything so forthright when he approached the leaders of the city. In his experience, few of the people on this young world were ready to admit that there might be such a thing as magic. Everyone knew the gods had ordained the existence of the worlds, and that the titans had crafted them out of their own magical essence, but few were prepared to face the unvarnished truth that the power behind that creation was still alive and well.

Few challenged the power and wisdom of the druids, who spoke to the spirits of the world. Most people had some first-hand experience of a druid conversing with the wind, or questioning a hill.

Fewer still doubted the all-too-evident blessings some people were granted by anima-spirits. Every village, every tribe had a totem-warrior or a healing-shaman of one sort or another. Only in the large cities were these absent. But even city dwellers had contact with the people of the countryside, the hunters, nomads, tribal warriors, forest hermits and nature priests.

It was difficult for anyone to deny that a warrior blessed by the rhino-totem could smash whole ranks of enemy soldiers, or that a healer chosen by a forest spirit could heal wounds in days or hours that would otherwise prove fatal. So, forced by experience, these were believed.

But sorcery and wizardry were rare, and often hidden. Even when acknowledged, they were often seen as inhuman things, blasphemously stolen from the titans and the gods. Mortal men feared what they could not comprehend, and, fumbling for a way to deal with it, often resorted to simple denial.

It was, after all, much easier to pretend wizardry didn't exist than to admit it and be forced to confront the fact that there were people in the world who could shape reality to their will and deny the natural order of the world. So Gem was used to people ignoring his peculiar abilities.

He reached into the lady's mind, much as he had with young Casu.

In Casu, he had read questions, fears, profound levels of confusion and ignorance. He had found the surface sloth and greed and lust that was so common in undisciplined youth, but he had also found a core of decency and an almost-smothered urge towards honor. So he fed the flame of that deep core and led Casu towards the thoughts that would awaken the flame of nobility within him.

In Lady Urula, Gem's strange powers found a mind that had all the potential to become a truly masterful wizard, but none of the discipline and training necessary for it. Beyond the raw potential, she had determination, cunning, curiosity, the ripe intelligence of a born scholar. He also saw the vanity at her core, but such was alien enough to him that he passed over it without real understanding.

In her, he saw a potential apprentice such as he had never had. Someone who could, given the right inspiration and guidance, work at his side at mastering the raw chaos of magic itself. A spark of hope lit in the loneliness that was his lot in a human world.

Like every aware being, human or elf or anything else, he longed for someone who could understand him as he was, to whom he could speak openly and with real understanding. The lady lit that hope as no one had ever done before.

Mere moments had passed in his introspection, such was the speed and skill of his mastery of minds – his own and others.

"I can win this battle, my lady. For you, I will charge one of two prices, as you see fit. Either ten pounds of sovereign gold, or a boon of trust from you. If you choose the latter, there are secrets that I think you will find profitable to know. What I ask will not be easy, but will compromise neither your honor nor your position. I will not say more at this time, and do not require an answer till after the battle."

He continued, "There are conditions on my service on the battlefield…" It took them some time to go over the details of his plans, such as he would reveal to her at that time, and to answer her questions, however vaguely in some cases, about his strictures and his service.

When all was said and all was agreed, Gem and Casu left little more than hour after they had arrived.

Within minutes of their departure, messengers had been sent out over the city to invite the other noble lords to meet with the lady.

They would use the same neutral building as before. The lords and ladies of Xalax were as short on trust as they were long on wealth, and none would meet where any other had the advantage of more guards or lockable rooms.

She made it clear the meeting was urgent, and gave them only till the next night to prepare for it. They had their spies in the city, just as she did, and in her household, as she had in theirs. They would know little less than she by the time they met, and that was good enough.

When the nobles had gathered, the same crowd as before, Lady Urula told them of Gem's contract.

"He and his men will meet the horde and defeat it two weeks hence, when it comes within the lands we of Xalax own. He demands that his army be the only one on the field, though we may guard our city as we see fit and with whomever we desire. He was quite clear on that demand, and will consider the whole contract void if we violate it."

Several of the nobles expressed their contempt at the idea that a common soldier, one who sold his services to the highest bidder, would try to dictate terms to them. Lady Urula insisted that he was adamant about it.

"How large is his army?" asked one of the lords.

"Himself and eight men," was the lady's reply.

The result of this pronouncement was as close to mob-panic as a crowd of that sort could get.

"Are you mad?" demanded one lady. "We understood you were buying an army to defend us! We haven't time left to arrange a real army, now that you've wasted all the time since the horde turned our way!"

Lady Urula sneered at them. "I can tell the good captain that he need not defend your homes and lands, and keep his services to my own properties, if you like."

The following argument resulted in three challenges to duels, a dozen pronouncements that the city was doomed, and several nobles leaving in full huff.

By the time the meeting was done, everyone had agreed to field no other armed men in Gem's chosen battlefield. This was an easy agreement to achieve, since none had men to spare from guarding their own homes.

Lord Uffney had the last word as everyone filtered out of the meeting and headed home. "Lady, your captain and his men will spend their time whoring and drinking for the next two weeks. Then they will either die bravely but uselessly, or abandon us and flee to the north, while the horde loots, rapes and pillages all of our lands and people. It is your money to waste, since you hired them, but I truly wish you hadn't given us false hope by promising an army.

"I won't flee," he continued. "My family has been in Xalax since the Days of Creation, twelve generations of lords and ladies, and there have never been cowards in it. But that will be cold comfort when we're all dead or enslaved. Good night lady. For your sake, I hope you die bravely in your house, and don't end up enslaved or raped to death." It was as generous as he could be through the rage in his heart.

Chapter 3: Can It Even be Called War?

When the Death Horde of Trialak came to challenge the Lady of Xalax, she called upon the Light of the Void itself, and wove magic so masterful, so wonderful, so exquisite of design and form, that wizards wept when they saw it. That something so beautiful would be used for war is a bitter lesson on the nature of magic itself. Power and temptation are easily twisted to destruction by anyone unwise. But the Lady had wisdom, and her might prevailed against the false power of the Horde. –
from the official histories of Xalax

The prostitute's name was Ulla, and she was *enjoying* sex for the first time in her life. Though she had given her body to hundreds of men, never before had it been anything other than hard work.

She had started out naturally drawn to the captain's exotic looks – his black skin and pale eyes intrigued her from the moment she first saw him. She was being paid to flirt with him and seduce him, but she was sure she would have done the same even without money if she were ever in a situation where she had a choice about such things.

When the captain got back from whatever errand he'd gone on, most of his men were already asleep in their rooms. Some with the lady or ladies of their choice, others drunk and alone, as each preferred. A few of the women, including Ulla, had been told to wait for the captain's return.

They didn't mind spending the evening waiting in the common room and being paid generously for nothing but sitting and gossiping with each other. Even with the looks and rumors they inspired in the inn's other customers, it was preferable to their usual evenings.

When Gem returned from his meeting with Lady Urula, all of them greeted him warmly and flirted with him. That was their job, after all. But for Ulla, it hadn't just been work – she found she actually liked the captain and was oddly but undeniably attracted to him.

She was genuinely pleased when he picked her out of the handful of women available to him.

She was unsurprised when he spent the first hour or so conversing with her. Many men spent much of their time with her talking about the things in their lives that nobody else would listen to. But it was unusual that he spent as much or more time listening to her than talking to her. That he was interested, and not just morbidly curious, was unusual enough, but it was truly unique that he was interested enough to take time to draw her true story forth.

After a while, it was a natural progression from conversation to seduction. He was a good kisser, and paid real attention to her during the whole seduction. Despite her profession, she had very little experience in dealing with a man who didn't just skip straight from "here's your money" to "I like to be on top". Talking was usually after. Or men would just fall asleep. Or send her away.

Her pimp had a tough enough reputation, and enough idea of the value of his "assets", that men didn't dare hit her or hurt her enough to leave bruises or marks. But simply "not hurting" was a vast distance from being nice or caring.

Gem had started with skillful foreplay. Ulla had never before experienced a body-shaking orgasm, so it was as unexpected as it was welcome when Gem made sure she hit that height before attending to his own needs.

Now she was on her hands and knees, the captain kneeling behind her, and she could tell that both of them were rapidly approaching their peak.

Outside the room, and outside Ulla's focused attention, three men stood in the hall and whispered plans of blood and money.

"Ener, you and me gonna kill him. Ber, you kill the girl," said Tep, the leader of the trio.

Ber objected quietly. "Why I gotta kill the girl, Tep? She's Deller's property, and he'll skin me alive if he finds out I killed one of his pretties."

Tep sneered. "Don't be stupid! We rob this guy, then we run north. The horde's coming through town, and Deller and ev'yone else 'ill be too busy being dead to kill you!" he snarled quietly.

Ber thought about it a long moment, then decided that even Deller probably couldn't kill someone when he was dead from barbarians.

He nodded his assent, and the three snuck up to the curtained doorway to Gem's rented room.

All three had heard rumors of the captain having a fortune. The legend had started with a single gold coin to Kon, and had grown to Gem throwing around handfuls of gold and having more money than most lords. Larceny was inevitable, and it had incarnated itself in the form of three thugs named Tep, Ber, and Ener.

Normally, they preyed on the streets. Slitting the throats of the not-quite-moneyless and robbing them of anything of value was their trade.

They never paid for any of the city's many prostitutes, preferring rape. They didn't much care what sex or age their victims were, nor whether their victims were particularly healthy or even clean. All three crawled with parasites and smelled of rot.

The smell was amplified by the cheap booze they guzzled whenever they could steal or afford it.

As they arrived at the doorway to their fortunes, they heard a woman's voice in the room breathlessly moaning about how filled up she was.

Ener whispered to Tep, "Can I watch fer a minute before we kill them? I ain't never heard a woman moan like that – I bet he's huge and I wanna see it!"

Tep glared at him till he shut up. They were going to be rich, and they didn't have time for a show to get in the way of the money!

As was common in that land, the room had only a heavy curtain in the doorway, not a solid door. As soon as his compatriots were quiet and ready, Tep doused the light in the hall and pushed the curtain aside.

The only light in the room came from moonlight through a paper-paned window. Tep could only just make out the shape of the bed in the dark, and the two writhing forms on it were barely visible.

He heard a slight noise from Ber as they stepped into the room, but the sound was drowned out by the slapping of flesh-on-flesh and the heavy breathing and moaning of the pair on the bed.

As he crept in, Tep felt a momentary pressure against his neck, a feather-touch along a thread-fine line below his jaw, without pain or shock.

Suddenly, something wasn't right. Breathing felt heavy and hard. He tasted blood and he couldn't swallow because something was wrong with his throat. He almost didn't have time to wonder why he couldn't see anything anymore before he barely felt his knees hit the floor. He was dead before he flopped down between his two dead friends.

Ulla was coming down from the most incredible sensation of her young life when she heard three sodden thuds from the doorway to the room. Gem had finished before her, and pulled out as she began to relax.

She wondered what the thuds were, but the captain seemed unconcerned about it as he backed away from her. He ran his hands gently over her one last time, drawing a final frisson from her as he withdrew. Then he stepped out of the bed and she stretched out and relaxed, satiated and filled with pleasant lassitude.

Light flooded the room as the lamp and several candles spontaneously lit themselves. She didn't see how he could have done that, but she forgot to care when she saw the three dead bodies lying in growing pools of blood in the entry to the room!

Her scream brought Gem's men, Kon, and several others running.

Soon, the inn was crawling with officials and city guards and the merely curious. The commotion drew a crowd outside and in.

Kon was shrieking about murder in his rooms and guests being assailed in their sleep by rampaging criminals.

A captain of the city guard was asking everyone questions and making stern-faced accusations, equally sure that each person present was "the one who caused this heinous crime".

Goreg, one of Gem's soldiers, was helping Casu recover from vomiting.

Ulla cowered in Gem's arms, both of them sitting naked on the bed. She didn't notice when there was an increase in the noise and disturbance at the front of the inn.

The commotion spread up the stairs to the second floor and then came into the hall that led to Gem's room. It was Lady Urula and a half-dozen of her bodyguards!

The lady's hair was still braided for sleep, and she was dressed in nightclothes, while her guards wore heavy leather armor with bronze and steel plates and rivets and carried their long daggers openly in their hands. It was a bizarre mix of suddenly-awakened and heavily-armed, noble-not-ready-to-be-awake surrounded by Amazonian-prepared-for-war.

Gem's men went from standing around or being useful, to combat-ready between one heartbeat and the next. They didn't know who this lady was, but she brought a large number of armed soldiers with her who looked like they meant business.

Gem glanced at the scene. Without a word being said, his men stood down and bowed to the lady in the nightgown, as if her half-dressed presence were the most normal thing in the world.

Casu and Kon, who recognized the lady, were busy kowtowing on their knees, suddenly regardless of the bloody floor and the dead lying on it.

The guard captain bowed deeply and tried to speak to the lady, but she and her guards brushed him aside.

She took in the sight of the bodies in the doorway to the room. She saw Gem and a panic-stricken woman naked in the bed. Nobody had to tell her what had happened.

She addressed the guard captain. "Captain. Make sure this was merely an attempted robbery. If these men," she indicated the three corpses, "were hired by my rivals, I want to know it by sunrise. The soldier and his men are the only hope our city has of living through the next month. You and your men will make them safe by whatever means necessary."

She didn't bother to ask if he understood. She didn't stop to find out if he would obey. She merely raised an eyebrow at Gem, as if to ask if there was anything she needed to know. He shook his head briefly.

With one last imperious glance, Lady Urula swept out of the inn and disappeared into the coach that had brought her.

Since Kon was still in a state of shock, Gem took charge. In moments, he had his men carrying the bodies out of the room and cleaning up the blood and vomit from the hall and floor. As soon as they could leave without wading through blood, he took Ulla to another room and got one of the inn's slaves to bring her some hot food and strong wine. He comforted her till she'd eaten, drunk, and passed out, then he called his men to him.

In a private room, they gathered around him.

"It was just a robbery attempt," he told them. "No spies, no assassins, just common thieves."

He touched each man briefly on the forehead with his finger, and fatigue vanished from them. "You men won't need to sleep tonight. Spread out and make sure the word hits the streets that a dozen robbers tried to kill us in our sleep and died for it. I want rumors of hacked corpses, slashed to ribbons by swords and knives. Go."

They understood, and they went.

For the next two weeks, the reputation of Gem and his men was that they were fiends straight out of Hell. Dozens of robbers and bandits had stormed the inn, and had died in vain. Gem was as rich as several lords put together, but the money was safe because dead men spend no fortunes.

Some of the city lords and ladies, hearing these rumors, approached Lady Urula with cautious overtures of possible reconciliation. They were still mostly convinced the city was doomed, but a few entertained a shred of doubt and the faintest glimmer of hope.

The city guards and the militia discovered that the streets near the Red Rooster were uncompromisingly crime-free while Gem was there. The usual pickpockets, muggers, and sundry other thieves and burglars were either lying low or had left for safer hunting grounds.

The streams of refugees heading north from the city slowed to a trickle as the day of the battle approached. Everyone who hoped that leaving would keep them safe was long gone. Everyone still in Xalax either had the insane hope that fighting would work, or held that fleeing and staying were both apathetically doomed and there was no real choice between the two fates.

The night before Gem was scheduled to ride out to meet the invading horde, Lady Urula called on him one more time. She caused quite a commotion by coming, for the second time, to the inn, instead of calling him to her. Some saw it as inappropriate that a noble lady would visit a mere mercenary captain in a common inn. Others gossiped that Gem and his men were demons and she was drawn to their dark power and in their unholy sway. A few wondered quietly if perhaps the lady was having another of her infamous affairs, this time with the mercenary captain.

She met him privately again. No guards to overhear what was said or done.

"Captain, I have something for you. I think you may be able to use it," she said. She handed him a small opal.

"I don't know how to describe what I did to it. But if you think at it and will me to know what you think, the stone can bind a message that only I can read."

Gem looked at the small gemstone. He smiled. "You bound the essence of your thought into it. It's an interesting trick. I've never seen it before, but it's obvious now that you showed it to me." He nodded in approval, and looked back from the stone to the lady.

She was staring at him like he'd grown horns and turned purple. She stammered, "I did what?"

He realized she truly didn't know what she was doing.

"Apologies, Lady. I thought you knew what you'd done." He paused a moment, then looked into her eyes. "You have strong barriers around the core of your thoughts. When we first met, I thought you had a sorcerer in your employ who was shielding you. Now I see ... hmmmm"

He paused a moment, then spoke quietly and with a strange emphasis. "Lady, what do stars look like to you?"

Lady Urula was surprised by the question. "Stars? I don't know what you mean, Captain!"

He nodded to himself, but spoke to her. "I think you do know what I mean." He repeated his question, determined for her to answer. "What do stars look like to you?"

The lady blushed and realized her evasion wasn't going to succeed. She was looking at the floor and her face was slightly pale when she realized she had to answer and quietly said, "I've never seen the sparks of light in the night sky that other people speak of. I see a sky full of strange worlds. They look like ... islands in a sea of air and clouds. You may think me insane, but they truly do."

His response shocked her. He smiled broadly, but it wasn't the mocking smirk she'd expected. It was the first time she'd seen actual happiness on his normally taciturn face.

"Lady, you need to go east to Sam's Tower. There, you will find others who see the world-shards for what they are. First, you should know that, far from insane, you are one of the few who sees Creation in its raw form, without the comforting lie that stars are distant points of light. Second, you must know that this will destroy you if you don't learn to master it. You must travel for a time to Sam's Tower, in the furthest East, where the Masters will teach you to control your gift."

She stared at him wide-eyed. "Travel? I cannot leave my lands unmanaged. If you drive off ... when you drive off the invading horde, I will need to manage my family holdings, or I will lose them to my rivals among the nobility of the city. Xalax has always been that way and always will."

Gem shrugged off her objections. "What you will learn in the far east, across the ocean and on the far side of the furthest continent, will make political infighting over a few square feet of land seem truly petty indeed. If you survive your training and master your gift, you can choose to return to Xalax as its undisputable ruler. But you may find that tedious after you learn real power."

He saw he hadn't fully convinced her. "We will talk again tomorrow. After the horde has been defeated, when we discuss your choice of payment."

The lady didn't know how Gem was going to rout the invading horde. But somehow her last lingering doubts were gone. She knew they would, indeed, speak again the next day, after the battle.

Lady Urula left the inn and went home. She had things to ponder and mysteries to wonder about. All the way home, she stared out the window of her carriage, at the worlds and parts of worlds that filled the sky.

Before the sun rose, Gem and his men rode south from Xalax. They left Casu and Ulla behind at the inn, with most of their meager possessions and a few words of encouragement. Casu, Ulla and Kon all felt as most in the city did, that this was their last day in Xalax. The horde was mere miles away, and would arrive at the city palisades before noon.

It was clear to everyone that the palisades and partial walls would barely slow the invaders, if even that much. They were a desperate gesture by desperate people. Most were determined to die fighting, or at least standing on their own two feet on land they considered theirs. A few were so apathetic that they simply expected to die or be enslaved and it made little difference which. A few more regretted that they had waited till it was much too late to run. Only one person in the city had true hope that today would see the end of an existential threat to their city.

Gem, Andwer, Saluem, Kethen, Goreg, Mithoty, Liwilam, Milaech, and Nathe, rode a dozen miles south of Xalax, then dismounted and tied their horses to stakes they had brought with them.

The horde was already awake and on the move, less than a mile south of them. Over a hundred-thousand strong, they made so much noise that Gem and his men could hear them faintly even at that distance.

The eight men stripped, all but Gem. They laid their armor and weapons in piles on small sheets of waterproofed canvas.

Gem adjusted his heavy plate-armor and pulled on heavy gauntlets and a simple helmet. In a world where cured leather with bronze strips over vital areas was considered heavy armor, he was wearing eighty pounds of steel plates, with chain-link-mesh under the heavy sheet-metal, and a layer of heavy bull-hide sewn to pads of soft cotton that pressed directly on his skin.

Finally, they were all ready. His men as naked as at birth, and Gem dressed like a mobile fortress.

Gem held his large sword out in front of him. Most men would have had trouble keeping ten pounds of steel steady at arm's length, but the blade and his arm could have been those of a statue for all the motion in them.

His men gathered in front of him around the extended sword. Each reached out his left hand and rested it on the horizontal flat of the blade. Fevered excitement filled their eyes and they had to swallow as anticipation moistened their mouths.

Gem's face was as blank and still as carved granite as they gathered.

When the last placed his hand on the extended sword, blue light filled Gem's eyes.

A pulse of pale blue energy coursed down the blade, from cross-piece to tip. It writhed through shapes that were there-and-gone too fast for human eyes to see the intricate runes the unnatural energy wrote on the fabric of reality.

The men growled.

The pulse repeated its path down the heavy blade. Over and over, flickering from hilt to tip.

As it grew faster and steadier, it matched to their hearts, and the men's bodies filled with a strange light.

As the pulsing light filled them, they grew and warped.

In moments, the eight stood transmogrified. Ten feet tall, covered with bark-like skin, with crowns of small horns around the tops of their monstrous heads, they were no longer human. Their arms and legs elongated and distended muscles writhed under armored skin. Their faces stretched into animal-like muzzles with predatory jaws and monstrous fangs. Foot-long saberteeth jutted from their jaws. Acidic poison dripped from razor-sharp talons on the ends of their nightmarish fingers.

They didn't need words to know their roles in Gem's plan. With a thunderous howl, all their voices joined in a single inhuman sound, they split into two groups of four and charged towards the far flanks of the approaching horde.

Their job was to herd the enemy towards Gem.

Gem lowered his sword and held it at a low angle in one hand. He walked with a determined pace towards the center of the oncoming army. Where it was at its densest. The most dangerous part of the battlefield.

His stride ate up the distance till the horde caught sight of him. Tens of thousands of blood-crazed warriors shouted as they saw the lone soldier marching towards them.

As one, they surged forward, fury and hunger driving them towards Gem!

Warriors infused with the power of a thousand spirit-totems charged towards their first victim of the day.

Serpent warriors hissed their fury. Lions and tigers roared their battle-cries. A few dozen blessed by the spirits of elephants and rhinos stampeded to trample him.

His march was a metronome of steady motion.

Then they were at bow-range and a thousand missiles leapt ahead of frenzied infantry.

Mid-air, the arrows disintegrated into splinters and dust.

Gem gestured, and suddenly the front rank of warriors turned on each other and began to rend and tear each others' flesh!

Some men dropped weapons and tried to kill their companions with teeth and fingers!

Others slashed spears and knives at their erstwhile allies.

A dozen charged Gem and struck him with all their might.

Everything that touched his armor exploded! Titanic blasts threw mangled warriors through the air, their bodies shredded by fragments of their own shattered weaponry.

In moments, thousands of dead littered the ground ahead of Gem. Thousands more lay bleeding and rent. Some of the wounded kept trying to kill everything near them, tearing their own ravaged bodies in their frenzy.

Gem's slow pace was immutable.

In a growing wave centered on his steady form, warriors stopped whatever they were doing and went insane. They lashed out at friends, companions, even lovers. The frenzy spread like wildfire!

Screams of rage and terror filled the air. The clash of arms and the cries of the wounded drowned out the whimpers of the dying.

Gem kept walking, an implacable force of absolute insanity and destruction.

Here and there, a few of the fearless with unbreakable wills struggled free of the aura of berserk fury. They attacked the death god who was killing their companions by the thousands. And they were destroyed as soon as their courage gave them the chance to touch him by hand or by weapon.

Unscathed, unstoppable, absolute in his deadly command of the battleground, Gem strode on.

Arrows and spears blackened the sky around him. Some found allied victims, adding to the carnage no army of this world had ever seen. Most hit the ground around Gem harmlessly. A few disintegrated in flight before coming anywhere near him.

Gem was determined to destroy the cause of this horde. Not just the immediate threat, but also the power that had created the threat in the first place.

The thing that had fueled the conquest and destruction of a hundred cities had to be destroyed. There would be no mercy for the one who had used forbidden power to drive these barbarians into actions that had finally forced Gem's hand. He could not let them destroy civilization in his world. No cost was too great for stopping them, but he meant that those behind the calamity would pay, not just their witless minions and dupes.

He knew where to look. He knew exactly where every mind was on the whole battlefield. Not a thought escaped his supernatural awareness. His true enemies were hiding behind thousands that they considered expendable, but he was on his way to them. They would meet his wrath.

Finally, a large man in bizarre dress, with a twisted black staff of wood that wasn't from this world, was before him. The man was afraid, but also confident of his power. The staff gave him command over every living thing he'd ever met, and he was sure he could defeat this lone foe as he'd defeated every enemy before.

Two last warriors stood between Gem and the staff wielder. They weren't barbarian spirit-warriors like those that filled the blasted pit of carnage behind Gem. These were different.

The light of creation suffused them as they raced to face Gem. They were beautiful, even in their rage, and imbued with such grace, strength and speed as no mortal human could aspire to. Their elvish magic shielded them from Gem's mental commands, and they charged towards him at inhuman speed.

Their spears were protected against the aegis of Gem's armor.

It was the fight he most hated to win.

Spears danced towards the weak points of his armor. For the first time, Gem moved as a fighting man. Faster even than elvish reflexes, he parried one spear with his sword, and deflected the other with his armored left hand.

A step too fast for eyes to follow. A slash with enchanted steel. One spear was cut off a hair's breadth from its owner's hand.

Another darting move and he was inside the reach of the second elf. Too fast to see, he slammed his armored fist into the elf's beautiful face. Bones shattered and the elf was driven to the ground, unconscious and mangled.

The other elf moved too fast for Gem to control the fight. He had no choice but to defend with his sword, and he left the elf skewered and bleeding, his heart sliced in two.

He hated to harm such beauty as elves. They were as close as humanity came to perfection, and hurting them, maiming them, twisted his heart with anguish.

One lay unconscious and bleeding, his face smashed and his neck broken. The other was barely breathing as blood from his shattered heart filled his chest and collapsed his lungs.

Gem knew they would take years to heal from those wounds. It was truly awful what they would suffer while they recovered. He regretted every second of pain he had inflicted on them. But at least he hadn't had to kill them – he had prevented at least that last tiny fraction of sin.

But the man with the black staff was attacking him now. No more soldiers. No more bodyguards. Just the magic of the staff against Gem's own knowledge and power.

The staff contained something dark. Something Gem had never seen before. The magic in it was … he flinched when he saw that the staff was an incarnation of death itself. He had never known that the very essence of death could be part of magic.

Power crashed into power in a battle no mortal eyes could see. One would have mastery, the other would be erased from existence.

An eyeblink was eternity itself compared to the time Gem's power wrestled with the power of the staff, and then the staff was unmade, the only remnant a dark scar in Gem's soul. A price he would pay to shield the world he loved from unbearable darkness.

Air cracked in sudden thunder as it rushed into the void left where the staff had been! The shaman was empty-handed and facing the monster that had destroyed his whole army, defeated his elvish slaves, and unmade the source of all of his once-immense power!

The last thing he ever saw was Gem making the slightest motion with his hand. The last thing he ever felt with a thread of pure force severing his head from his neck. It felt like something pressed lightly against his neck, and then it felt like nothing at all.

Chapter 4: Dragon On

The world was still young when word arrived of the death of the dragons and the destruction of Dragonhome. Every rumor spawned a thousand children and they a thousand grandchildren each, but none truly knew how Death had visited the bastion of the most powerful immortals.

*Ariel, last of the dragons, lost and
forlorn, battle-weary and crippled, was
taken in by the Lady Magistrix, in her
compassion.*

*In the presence of the Lady, a
miracle came to be! Beseeched by the
Lady, even the gods felt that Her wisdom
was the only hope for the world, and,
bereft of all other hope, they bowed to the
Lady's will and reached into the world to
make Ariel the first and only Dragon
Wizard! An avenger for her kind and her
home, when the vile gnomes sought to
bring their war and their world-destruction
to the Lady's lands! – <u>from the official
histories of Xalax</u>*

Lieutenant Charther was huddling in the lower guard tower on the pass known as The Gate of Wizards, high in the mountains known as the Pillars of the Gods. Thundersnow raged around the tower, cold enough to kill a man in minutes, even one dressed for the usual chill of the high pass. Inside, secure from the biting wind and sheltered from the occasional blast of lightning, it was still cold enough to make him shiver. The fireplace valiantly fought to keep the tower habitable, but it was one of those battles that neither side ever wins. Outside, it was so cold the mercury in the thermometer had long-since frozen solid.

The men in the upper tower would be warm and secure. No merely natural storm could disturb the magic of the flying structure. Charther didn't understand why the lower tower couldn't also be warded, but supposed that if he could understand, he'd be a wizard instead of a border-guard, and wouldn't be in the tower or, for that matter, care whether it was warm or cold.

He sat his watch alone. No reason to make any of his men suffer with him. They'd take over in a few hours, and then he could go to the upper tower and be warm while one of them slowly froze. He was pretty sure it was Jessal's shift next, but didn't really care much. In this weather, keeping a watch on the pass was surely entirely pointless. The suffering was needless, but the lords of the city would be angry if they failed to keep at least someone on-duty at all times.

He was probably correct in his assumption that anything that could invade the pass during the storm wouldn't really be deterred by mortal guards, no matter how impressive their magical tower was, nor how duty-bound their freezing commander.

Thus, he was shocked and alarmed when the entry-bell rang. Someone was in the foyer!

The outer door was made to open from the outside. It was never locked, but the latch on it required hands to open. No wind or wild animal would be able to get into the entry-room of the tower!

The bell was rigged to ring automatically when anyone entered the room. Guards could peer into the room through a mirror-contrivance that wasn't magical, but did allow seeing into the room without exposing oneself to threats from anyone in there. The bell meant he needed to look.

How could anyone be in there in this weather? It made no sense!

For a moment, Charther considered calling for backup from the upper tower. Then he dismissed it. If whoever was out there was in dire straits, it might take too long for help to arrive. And why pull them from their warmth and comfort if he didn't need to? And if whoever was out there was somehow powerful enough to be safe in this storm, a druid or elf or some such, an extra guard or six wouldn't do him any good anyway. Maybe whatever it was would just kill him, and then he wouldn't be cold anymore!

He chuckled momentarily at his own morbid humor, then shook off his trepidation and, muscles stiff from long sitting in the chilly room, he stood and walked to the viewing apparatus. It took his shivering, half-numb fingers a moment to open the lens.

It was a person. Definitely that. Details were concealed by heavy furs and a dark cloak and hood, but he could tell that it had a human shape. Could be an elf, of course, but what would one of them be doing here? Far too small for a troll, though he had an impression of height even through the uncertainty of the mirrors and prisms. So, alone and probably human.

He paused. Again, the feeling that there was something beyond his judgement here was strong. One person, heavily dressed, coming out of the storm and into the tower, was hardly likely to be a serious threat, and might be someone in desperate need of help. But he hesitated as some instinct told him this was dangerous.

He clamped down his willpower and summoned his courage out from the corner it seemed to be cowering in, and decided he had best act fast.

Whoever it was, they didn't look like they were dying at that very moment, so he took a moment to send a quick message to the upper tower. He told the men there what he had seen, and warned them not to come down to the lower tower till either he had sent an all-clear, or to come in force, expecting trouble, in five minutes, if they hadn't heard from him by then.

That angle covered, he closed the viewer and lifted the bar from the inner door. The outer door would not open while the inner was unbarred, so he felt at least that degree safe. It would just be him and the stranger from the storm. No one else.

He picked up his shield and short-spear and pulled the chain that would open the inner door.

A blast of hideously cold air hit him in the face, and he saw the mist of his breath whip away. But it was just the one quick burst. The person in the foyer looked at him patiently as he stood there, spear and shield at the ready, and the person said nothing.

For a moment, they stood still, facing each other. He couldn't make out any details through the heavy clothing, and the person's face was covered almost entirely by the collar of the cloak. What he could see were golden eyes. Somehow infinitely feminine, with irises of warm gold, long, pale lashes, and fine eyebrows. The bridge of her nose was delicate. He began to think of the stranger as "her" even though he couldn't see any definite proof of that.

She was taller than he, but he couldn't tell anything more about her general build or shape beyond that in the heavy clothing she wore.

He faced her for just a moment, and then decided he needed to either let her all the way in, or kick her all the way out. With the inner door open, the already cool room was chilling further every second!

"Come in, traveler. Come in and be welcome to the outmost rampart of Xalax," he spoke the traditional words. He gestured with the spear and ushered her into the main room. As soon as she stepped in, he shut the door and closed the bar on it, sealing out the rest of the storm.

Most lonely travelers would have been staring at the spear. It was an open threat, even if his words were ones of welcome. Xalax had been at war with several of its neighbors for longer than anyone could remember, and it had to guard its borders with magic and steel. But that didn't make it polite. It was a threat, and most people would have at least looked at it. But not her. Her eyes never left his.

She reached up and pulled back her hood and mask. Charther gasped! She was beautiful! He'd seen a few elvish women before, and held them to be the ideal of perfection and beauty, but this woman somehow outshone even them!

When she spoke, her voice was a smoky, sexy contralto. He barely heard her words, he was so instantly hypnotized by the sound. After a moment, he realized he needed to answer her and desperately thought back to what she'd said.

"Is this Xalax?" had been her question.

"Well," he stammered, "it's part of Xalax. Sort of. We're the guards for Xalax, but the city is really several days further north. Past the mountains."

Charther was staring, and couldn't make himself stop. It wasn't just her beauty. She also had the strangest hair he'd ever seen. Instead of the common black of the local people, or the brown or orange of the distant northlands (he'd seen plenty of those people in his days as a guard on the western border before he was promoted to the officership over the pass-guard), or even the pale yellow-white of the barbarians of the Misty Isles, her hair was pale lavender with tips the subtle blue of a winter sky.

Of course! She was a wizard on her way to the school! Why hadn't he thought of that before? It all made sense. Some apprentice wizards could walk through fire, so it made sense that this one could survive weather that would kill a strong man in minutes. Most applicants to the school came in the summer, when the passes were safe, but that didn't mean they *had* to come at that time.

Reassured by this chain of reasoning, Charther relaxed and set the spear and shield down.

"You need the school, right?" he asked.

She looked at him blankly, then replied. "I need to speak with the wisest wizard in the world. I've been told to check in Xalax."

That made sense to him and he relaxed further. "Yes. Of course. The Lady Magistrix is the greatest wizard in the world. Everyone knows that. I don't know how you'd speak with her, but we can certainly help you talk to someone at the school. They'll know what to do."

She smiled and nodded, and Charther's heart leapt into his throat. He was in love with her and would do anything to help this amazing woman!

"Well then, I shall speak with someone at the school," she said.

His fingers fumbled in his haste, and he stammered a few words, but eventually he was able to use the messaging device to let the guards in the upper tower know that they needed to open the way for him and this lady to ascend to the upper tower, to use the communications room.

The upper tower was the real fortification. It floated, unsupported by physical means, in the air, sixty feet above the ground. It had thick walls of enchanted stone, further reinforced by bars and bands of mage-forged steel and bronze, with narrow slits for shooting arrows out of. The highest floor, nearly 100 feet above the ground, had telescopes inside narrow windows that could be sealed with metal shutters. The only entrance was through the bottom of the lowest floor – from which the inhabitants of the tower could "lower" a magical set of invisible stairs to a matching doorway in the roof of the lower tower. The stairs would only last a few minutes once conjured, and then anyone on them would fall.

Thus, the only ways in were through the lower tower, with the permission and invitation of those in the upper tower, or by flying through a fortified doorway in the floor of the upper tower, in the face of arrows, boiling oil, or anything else the guards up there felt like throwing or dropping on an intruder.

He guided her up the stairs towards the upper tower. At first, ordinary steps up the inside wall of the lower tower, but in a dozen steps, they were above the roof on the magical stairs. The storm raged around that stairway, but didn't touch it. There was no wall, but not a wisp of wind touched the stairs. No weather ever did for they had an invisible wall around them, of the same magical nature as the stairs themselves – solid to the touch though both sight and hearing were unimpeded by them.

He was used to guiding visitors' steps, since invisible stairs are difficult to navigate without experience, but she seemed unimpeded by this, and unimpressed even. Further proof to Charther's mind that she was a wizardling of some sort.

Normally, the view from the stairway was spectacular. During the day, the pass and the mountains were clearly visible all around. At night, the mountains became dim shapes, but the stars were points of diamond-brilliance. No one from the lowlands ever saw stars like those at these heights! Tonight, much as Charther wished he could show off the view, all that could be seen was the blast of snow all around.

Jessal met them at the door to the basement of the upper tower. He and Charther whispered secret passwords to each other, and then Jessal passed the two by and went down the stairs. His shift would start early this night, and he'd thus be cold longer, but his brief glimpse of the lady was the only thing on his mind as he descended to the cold lower tower.

All the men of the tower, a dozen all told, stopped what they were doing and stared. The lady took off her heavy outer garments and heavy boots and was dressed in a simple shift, peasant-leggings, and warm socks. This simple, baggy outfit should have hidden her shape. It was modest and demure, and it was sexier than lace and satin on anyone else. It covered everything, and merely added mystery to an obviously perfect body.

She was taller than any of the men, with long legs and a delicate, thin build that further emphasized her height. Her breasts were small, and the baggy shirt somehow drew attention to their perfect shape and flawless form. Most of the men had trouble tearing their eyes away from the slightest hint of the barest outline of a nipple.

Her face was lit from within by an ethereal, fine-boned beauty. Her exotic hair was either dismissed by the men as something that could be safely ignored in the presence of that much perfection, or as an exotic feature that added further to the art of her.

These border guards were young men who hadn't seen a living woman in months, and their behavior reflected that.

Charther took her to the communications room and led her to the orb. "Lady, I don't know if you can use this. If you can, you can reach the school directly. If not, they will call us in a few hours and you can speak with them then," he explained as he showed her the small, gemlike sphere that was the main line to the outside world most of the year.

She looked at the orb from several angles, and then put her right hand on it. A faint glow suffused the crystal ball, and she looked deeply into it. The glow waxed stronger for a few minutes, and then a masculine voice came from it.

"Who is this, please?"

She answered, "My name is Ariel. I need to speak with the Lady Magistrix."

There was the slightest pause. "You can't. She only speaks with the other master wizards. If you were one, you wouldn't be using a guard-tower sending-orb. So you can't speak to her. But you can speak with me. Are you coming to the school? Do you seek instruction?"

Ariel glanced a question at Charther. He smiled enthusiastically and nodded agreement.

Ariel spoke to the orb again. "Does one become a master wizard by coming to the school and seeking instruction?"

"Yes."

"Then that is what I will do."

"Good. Tell the guards to help you get here. We need every journeyman we can get. I look forward to seeing you." The glow faded rapidly.

Ariel looked to Charther. "Why do you think he said that about journeymen? I wish to become a master wizard, so I can speak with the Lady. Not a journeyman."

Charther was glad he could help her, even with this minor point. "An apprentice can't use the orb. A journeyman usually can. A master doesn't need one. I don't know much more than that, but that part was explained to me by a journeyman wizard who travelled through here last year and needed the orb to send a message to his master at the school." And thus a wizard's mistaken assumption changed the fate of a thousand worlds, for it never occurred to him that dragons could also use the orb, since he thought them all long-dead.

He went on to explain that Xalax had the oldest school of magic, and the Lady Magistrex, who ruled the city, was the most powerful wizard in the world. Many students went there every year. Although, he explained, they usually travelled during the summer, not the winter when the passes and roads were frozen and prone to storms.

Another city, named Tianan, far to the east, on the shore of the Great Eastern Ocean, had a larger school with more young students, but was less prestigious than Xalax and had no one who was as old and powerful as even the Lady's apprentices, much less the Lady herself.

So far away it was almost mythic was the city Loredon, on a misty isle in the mysterious Far West, on the edge of the world. Nobody knew more than rumors about it, and all of those were dark. Whispers of magic perverted for unnatural purposes swirled around Loredon, thick as the mists that were said to hide the city year-round.

There had, legends said, once been another wizard city south of Xalax, south of the pass, in the hot, exotic lands where the ancient horde of Trialak had once killed everything, before being destroyed by the Lady Magistrix. It had been founded, they said, by students of the Lady's school who had rebelled against her. Everyone agreed the wars with Xalax had destroyed that city and the lands around it, and none lived there now. It was as empty in the present as the ancient hordes had left it in legendary days.

Other cities, living cities, with powerful wizards ruling them, were said to exist in the vast lands across the Great Eastern Ocean. They brought the full number of cities to twelve, said all the legends, rumors and gossip, but nobody he'd ever met knew any of their names, places, or stories.

There were only two things everyone agreed on. First, that the wizards ruled the great cities and the cities, in turn, ruled the world and everything on it, from the boat-people of the southern seas to the frozen tundra of the far north, from the Lesser Western Ocean to the Great Eastern Ocean, and everything in between. Second, that the wizards all hated each other and fought unceasingly.

"And that's why we guard the borders. Though there's nothing ever going to invade from the south, we still have to watch.

And that's what this tower is for," he explained. She hadn't asked, but he would take any excuse to talk with her, and this was what he could think of.

Charther was disappointed when she told him she'd be travelling straight on. He argued that she should stay so he and the guards could help her get to Xalax, like the wizard said via the orb. They couldn't travel till the winter storms were done. And wasn't the pass too dangerous, even for her, at this time? Isn't that why she stopped at the tower for shelter?

"I must move on. My mission to the wizards is too urgent to wait. If I could fly, I would. But I can't, so I'll walk through the storm," she explained. She wouldn't say more about her mission, but merely insisted on leaving straight away.

Charther looked out the windows at the storm. In that rage of wind and ice, he or any of the guards would be dead before they were a hundred yards from the door. But he knew wizards, even journeyman wizards, played by different rules. A druid could convince the storm to leave, but there were no druids there to help him.

Not that he thought Ariel needed protecting. He was just lonely and she was beautiful. But he finally gave in and let her have her way. He helped her dress back up in her heavy furs. "It's what I'm supposed to wear in storms," she muttered in a way that sounded almost apologetic. As if she felt bad about making him help her bundle up, and would otherwise head out into the storm just in her thin peasant outfit. It made no sense to him, so he ignored it and finished tying her outfit shut.

Back in the cold, unpleasant lower tower, he ushered her into the foyer, and shut the inner door. The bell rang, and he looked into the viewer. She was gone, and he was sad that he'd never see her again. He hoped her magic would keep her alive in the storm. He'd heard that many young wizards burned themselves out by using magic they couldn't control. Some even died from it, if the rumors were true. He gave a quick prayer to the gods that Ariel wasn't one of those and that she would live through the storm.

Outside, Ariel quickly oriented herself by the stars and by dragon-instinct. The pass continued … that way. She glanced once at the tower, and felt sorry for the men inside it. Poor humans, she thought. Trapped in an artificial cave by a little frozen water and some mild breezes. Compared to some of the worlds she had visited with her father, where oxygen froze and hydrogen storms whipped winds at hundreds of miles per hour, the weather outside was barely even chilly.

The storm ended a few hours later. She was miles away from Charther's tower, and pressed on, tireless, inured to cold and wind, trying to look human in an environment where no human could have survived.

Over the days, as she travelled through the pass and into the northern lands, she saw more and more evidence of wizardry. The closer she got to Xalax, the more wizardry she saw. And all of it appeared to be aimed at warfare.

Hundreds of flying fortresses hovered over the land, some serviced by lower-towers and magical stairways like the one in the pass, some only entered by flying transports that looked somewhat like small boats.

From the foothills of the great mountains, she looked out over the lands to the north. Though she kept her human form, her eyes were still keen enough to see for hundreds of miles, and the land below her was full of people who were prepared for war. But not for the war she knew was coming their way.

She saw thousands of patrols marching hundreds of miles of roads and paths. Most of the soldiers she could see were human, but many were led by huge trolls, and even some of the humans showed signs of magical enhancement. At these distances (the nearest were dozens of miles away from the hill she stood atop), she couldn't see any details of the magic, but she could see where normal human auras had been enhanced, twisted, altered, by wizardry.

She continued downhill to the lower lands of the north. As she passed into them, she met many people, and talked with them to learn of the realm she had entered. In weeks of walking, she met and talked to people on the road with her, to people in inns and taverns, to farmers and their families. She avoided soldiers at first, since she wanted to learn more of the lands and people before she had to deal with military pride and the martial mindset.

She learned that the Lady Magistrix's personal soldiers were known as Battle Mages. They were men and women with too little magical talent to become actual wizards, but enough that the lady's power could make them into superhuman warriors. People she spoke with told tales of Battle Mages crafting enchanted weapons of fantastic potency, and of soldiers who could handily defeat such martial masters as even the elves could field. The greatest of them were said to be unbeatable by anything less than a troll.

When she felt ready, she let a military patrol find her on the road. She picked a small one, six men led by a single troll. She wanted them to be numerous enough to feel safe approaching her, but small enough that, if she had to kill them, they would be no great loss to Xalax's military might.

The human men of the patrol were heavily armed, with swords, spears and small but heavy bows, though they wore only light armor under their winter furs. Each of the cavalrymen led a spare horse by a long rope. They were boringly normal.

The leader, however, was obviously one of the trolls farmers and merchants had told her about. He walked next to the men, and, though they were on horseback, his head was nearly level with theirs. He was easily keeping up with the trotting horses, and drew the eye as the obvious threat, despite the cavalry at his back.

Ariel wasn't a good judge of human appearances. To her, all humans were somewhat plain, usually boring, frequently unattractive. But even she could tell the troll was ugly by human standards. To her, his predatory face, with uneven fangs and exaggerated features, merely spoke of a more efficient hunter. She guessed that humans would find him terrifying.

His rumbling bass voice was surprisingly pleasant. Though no humanoid body could render the deep resonances of a full-grown dragon, she still liked the ones with deep voices better than the squeaky ones. She had once heard a famous human singer, a woman who could shatter some types of glass with the notes of her voice. To Ariel, it had been more humorous than impressive.

"Miss," the troll addressed her, as they came parallel to her on the road and stopped. "Are you travelling alone?"

She nodded.

"It's not safe around here, miss. There are enemies of Xalax about. Are you heading to the school, or do you have other business in Xalax?"

"The school," she replied.

He nodded, looked around, and then made a decision. He looked at one of the cavalry with him, "Jaox, you'll go report to the station. Take two extra spares, and ride fast. When you get there, get fresh mounts and come back immediately. We're going to escort this young lady to the school."

Ariel tried to protest. "I'll be safe enough on the roads. I've come this far and …", but the troll interrupted her. "Miss, it's not safe, and we have to keep constant watch for enemies of the Lady and the city. It's obvious you're not from around here, and don't know the local lands, so it's important for us to escort you. To keep everyone safe."

Ariel realized that he wasn't escorting her for *her* safety. He dressed it up that way, but it was pretty obvious this was not an offer, but a demand. Her mission was to get their help, so fighting them wasn't a good option. She couldn't fly since the gnomes burned off her wings in the battle for Dragonhome, so escape also seemed unlikely. So she bowed to the inevitable and accepted the dignity the troll was trying to grant her in the process.

She might very well be a sort of captive, but at least her captor was being diplomatic about it. And she realized that this was probably her best opportunity to approach the school in a manner that the humans would find acceptable.

The troll introduced himself as Gregory. He also introduced his men, but Ariel found them strikingly boring and forgot their names as quickly as she was told them.

Gregory was a fairly typical troll. Nearly ten feet tall, weighing more than a medium horse, and strong enough to knock a horse off its feet in a single blow of his huge fist, he was pretty much average for his race. His skin was thicker and harder than that of a human, and covered in mottles and warts. His hair, hacked short by a knife instead of any sort of styling, was coarse, black, and lanky. But his most noticeable feature, compared to humans, was his gigantic, absolutely hideous face – a monstrous nose between bloodshot eyes, over a mouth that was more of a snout than otherwise, and with snaggly, uneven, razor-sharp teeth protruding between his heavy lips. Uneven lumps and scar-like pores covered most of his face, and patches of almost-fur covered much of the rest. Like most of the humans of that land, his hair was black, his eyes were dark brown, and his skin was mostly brown. The short, crude claws on his fingers and toes were barely noticeable given the rest of his demeanor.

Ariel knew, from descriptions, that trolls were fierce warriors, honorable, brave, immensely strong, and could recover from almost any wound so fast that almost nothing could kill them.

Gregory made it clear that he was going to be as polite as possible. Ariel suspected that his nose might be more sensitive than a human's, and not just larger, lumpier and hairier. If so, it was possible that he was treating her the way he did because of some sense of her draconic nature. Dogs, bears and other scent-predators often reacted to her much the way Gregory did.

Regardless, he walked with her and spent the time in conversation. Because he made the squad travel at a pace appropriate to a human woman walking, including numerous breaks and overnight rest, they had plenty of time to talk of many things.

Ariel was pleased to find that Gregory knew much of the history of the lands. Far more so than the simple farmers, peasants and merchants she had spoken with before meeting him.

When she asked about that, he responded, "Trolls are all warriors. The old wizards and Kamaia made us that way, and we're good at it. But we have long lives, like wizards, so we tend to pick up bits and pieces of lore along the way. We're not much for formal education, like they make young wizards do, but guard duty and sieges are both long on time and short on things to do, so we all end up studying sooner or later. It passes the time."

From him, she learned that Xalax was famous for three things. The first two were the Lady Magistrix, who was certainly the foremost wizard in all the world, and her school for wizards. The third was less interesting to Ariel, but it bore on Gregory's nature and she was curious about that. Xalax held a huge temple to twin sisters – magical spirits, said to be daughters of the world-titan. One was named Kamaia, the other had no name known to any mortal, and they were known all over the world for their twin abilities to heal any wound, any disease, in man or beast, and for their magical ability to make women pregnant.

Gregory explained that trolls thought of Kamaia as their mother. He told her that any women who made love and visited Kamaia for her blessing would have a healthy child. Even barren women, or women too old for children, could be blessed with a healthy baby by Kamaia and her sister.

Kamaia's symbol, he told her, was an eye lit by a wondrous green light from within. The temple had statues with emeralds for eyes in her honor. Her mysterious sister's symbol was a rose bush, and she allowed no statues or any other depiction of her likeness, but the temple had an amazing maze of roses behind it.

Ariel dismissed most of this as unimportant to her. She was far more interested in what little he knew of the school and the Lady. But she listened politely because it was obviously very important to Gregory.

Ariel originally intended merely to use Gregory as a source of information, but she found herself liking him. His soldiers were only good for flirting with her, and they were inept and overbearing at that. After her experiences with human military men, she began to wonder if they were deliberately bad at courting. Perhaps it was some sort of intentional tradition for them to be horrible at any sort of romance.

At the slow pace Gregory set, it took several days to reach the outer fortifications of Xalax proper. She spent most of the time listening to Gregory's stories about the centuries since his creation in Kamaia's temple. At times, she wished she could tell him some of her own stories. There were some that would have complimented his own memories and enriched his narrative with either shared experience or interesting contrast, but she held fast to her need to hide her true nature till she had secured the help of the world's greatest wizard. Telling him any of her past would have inevitably revealed her long life as a dragon, especially to an astute listener like Gregory.

Finally, they reached the city outskirts. The walls were built of cyclopean blocks of enchanted stone, and thickly plated with wizardrous bronze. The eternal patrols atop the walls, the unsleeping watch kept from titanic towers and flying platforms, the lake-size moats, and the narrow bridges that were the only access into the ancient city, were all martially effective. But Ariel saw nothing about them that would do more than give the gnomes pause. Why had her father sent her here? This looked helpless.

It took several interrogations by numerous guards to get her into the city. She was surprised that she was repeatedly asked, "What do stars look like?" Her answers were always deemed adequate, but she wondered at the import of the question. When asked details, like "What about that one?" or "Do you see any flaming stars overhead?", they always accepted her replies.

She didn't understand the questions, till a chance comment by Gregory convinced her that most humans could barely see stars, couldn't see them at all during the day, and were somehow deluded into seeing them as mere pinpricks of light in the night sky! It seemed to strange to her, but she had never thought to ask before, in any of her admittedly limited interactions with humankind.

She looked at the sky above her. It was filled with worlds, some so close she could see land and sea, mountains and oceans, others so distant she could barely make out what element dominated each. Most were made of elemental earth, usually with fire in the core and water and air pooled on the surface. Many of the rest were realms of air-storms, vast and chaotic and colorful. A few were formed almost exclusively of water, perhaps with a covering of air or a shell of ice. Fewest of all were worlds formed of fire, where heat and light and chaos ruled supreme.

She gathered, by what Gregory had said, that wizards could see stars the right way. It appeared that the point of the questions was to determine if she really was someone who belonged at the school, or if she was merely a pretty young woman whose strange hair had fooled someone into thinking she might be magical.

It was unimaginable to her that the sky could look any other way, but Gregory convinced her that most people, himself included, saw the sky as a nearly empty sphere above them. It might have a few clouds in it, and the sun and moon, but what she saw as worlds were, to him and the vast majority of humans, mere pinpricks of light that could only be seen at night, if at all.

It was nearly incomprehensible to her, but she accepted it because she trusted Gregory and knew he would not lie or tease about such a thing. He could only see three worlds, she finally understood – the one they stood on (and only a very small bit of that was visible to him, but the idea of a curve and a horizon were so alien she couldn't understand them at all), the extremely close dead world named "Moon", and the nearby fire-realm that lit the daytime sky as this world's "Sun". That both appeared as circles to him was more strangeness than she could grasp.

"You humans are weird," was her final statement on it. Gregory laughed and let it be.

When they were past the outer walls, and finally into the city itself, the most impressive thing about it was its crowded squalor. Human cities always came with a cloud of stink, but this was worse than normal. Far too many people living in far too small a space. Tanneries and smithies filling their air with smoke and worse, fishmongers and chandlers and butchers adding the smells of rot and blood to the place, the odor of hundreds of thousands of barely-washed human bodies all sweating and excreting and shedding hair and skin. And few thought to clean their mouths of the smell of years of tooth-rotting diets and alcohol. Over it all, the smell of inadequate sewer systems. And, of course, where you get human-stink, you always get dogs, cats, rats, pigs, goats, horses, cattle, and a hundred other species that all added to the miasma.

Fortunately for Ariel, while dragon noses are alert to every scent and can track better than dogs or even bears, they are also made to deal with irritants like swimming through seas of ammonia, and she was easily able to deal with the cloud of aerosol garbage that filled Xalax's streets. Her human-form nose would never support the level of detail her true form would, and wasn't nearly as tough, but it was adequate for this task, odious as it might be.

The air was only slightly less full than the streets. Gregory, by size and strength, was able to push his way through the shoulder-to-shoulder, face-to-armpit crowds. He was busy enough doing so that he never noticed that people simply parted around Ariel and she had a small but definite empty space around her.

The troll raised his voice to be heard over the immense noise of thousands of people. He had no way to know he didn't need to. Ariel's humanform ears were sensitive enough to hear him clearly. She still felt half-deaf with hearing that dull – in her real form, she could have heard him whisper from a block away, even with everyone on the streets shouting and bellowing.

Once past all the gates and security checkpoints, Gregory again became her guide, guard, and possible captor/jailor. As always, he was friendly and talkative.

He pointed out streets that she might need to know once she was allowed to leave the school grounds. He talked about the history of the city, and how it had once been much smaller and less important, till the wizards formed their alliance here and defeated the hordes of Trialak. The school was the natural result of the alliance. A few students, he said, were sent to The Tower, every few years. She could hear the capital letters in how he said it, and wondered what it might be.

"Nobody but wizards ever goes to The Tower. It's east of here. All the way at the farthest reaches of the world, I hear. Not sure what that means, since the world is round, but that's what the wizards say, and they won't say more than that."

Ariel didn't bother to correct him again about the world being round. They had already beaten that subject to an ugly death and there was no way to resurrect it gracefully.

"The ones that get sent there are the best students. The most powerful journeymen. They say that most don't survive their visit, but the ones who do return, centuries later, are the most powerful wizards. The Lady was the first to go there, and she's the one who decides who should go."

He pointed out a set of huge buildings in the middle of the city. "That's the temple to Kamaia and her nameless sister. Like I told you, it's the second center of power and influence in the city. Much less important than the Lady, but more important than just about anything else. It's mostly for druids, but anyone can go there for favors from the sisters, like we talked about. We trolls were made there, by an alliance of wizards and the demigoddess Kamaia, and we all visit her as if she were our mother."

Ariel was curious about the temple, but it didn't have anything to do with her mission, so she ignored it for the time being. If she had time, she could explore that mystery later. She focused on the school and the Lady. Everything else would have to wait.

Her dragon-senses did tell her that the temple, whatever it was to the humans, was a huge focus of power and attention for the spirits of this world. It might even be a channel to the world-titan, and that might prove useful later, in the war against the gnomes. But, mission first, world-titan and temple later.

Finally, after a long, guided tour, Gregory and Ariel arrived to the main entrance to the wizard academy. The wall around it was even higher, even more massive, than that around the city itself. The wall was a large semicircle, enclosing a half-mile-wide area at the foot of a large cliff. The cliff itself was heavily worked, with balconies and stairways and numerous rooms carved into its face. A river had been diverted around the base of the wall, forming a wide moat. The only bridge was made purely of magical force, like the stairs used between lower towers and the flying towers above them. The force of the bridge glowed with a faint, golden light, barely visible in the daylight.

The gate through the wall was immense. Big enough even for adult dragons, if they chose to walk through instead of fly over. The gateway and the gate were carved with many-detailed writings and images. The wall had many reliefs, inscriptions, sunk-reliefs, and every method of carving that could be imagined, stretching from end to end. Some of the work had been plated in gold or bronze, some had gemstones or ivory inlaid. A few bits were painted, but this was rare and the paint was faded, as painting the wall decorations was no longer fashionable and not being kept up or added to.

Deep in the stone and metal of the gate and the wall, Ariel could see that an immense amount of magic had been bound into the defenses of the school. No catapult would ever breach these walls merely by throwing rocks at it, no matter how forcefully. Elemental Earth had been fashioned by skilled wizards into something else here, something that would resist any natural force.

But the gnomish war machines were the very definition of a violation of nature. She feared the wall, however impressive it might be, was doomed, along with all inside it.

The moment she passed under the lintel over the gate, she noticed a difference. Where the city was loud, crowded, filthy, and odorous, the school was quiet, calmly and sparsely populated, clean, and smelled like fresh apples. Magical energy permeated everything in the school, even the dirt under the wide expanses of grass and trees.

One source of magic overwhelmed all the rest with its intensity and the depth of its power. She couldn't see where it was coming from, hidden behind several buildings. But the power of it pushed against her senses so forcefully it almost drowned out everything else in the school.

It took Ariel a few moments to realize that Gregory was turning her over to the school's guards. Six trolls, all heavily armed and armored, both physically and magically. She said a fond goodbye to Gregory, and he smiled, wished her well, and then he was gone.

The new guards didn't introduce themselves. They just herded her into a large room that was over-decorated even by dragon standards. Tasteless, gaudy, gilded statuary covered what looked like miles of shelves. The furniture was gold-plated and looked almost like it was designed to be as uncomfortable as possible while also blinding the eye and making any artist wince at the bad taste.

At the far end of the room, behind a desk so crusted with gemstones, ivory and precious metals that it was brighter than the lamps and windows around it, was a middle-aged human male. He was monstrously obese, sagging with fat and extra chins that failed to hide in a patchy beard that badly needed grooming and trimming. His clothing was cloth-of-gold, with imperial-purple silks and yet another encrustation of gemstones and pearls.

Ariel, as all dragons, had a strong streak of avarice. This much gold, this multitude of precious stones, even the rare wood that the desk had at its well-buried core, should have been enough to make her salivate in gold-lust. Instead, it was so tacky, so overdone, so artistically awful, that she sighed in pity and winced at the abuse of so much potential beauty.

The man glared at her and asked, in a voice that dripped arrogance and sarcasm, "So, you think you can sneak in here and spy on us?"

Ariel was momentarily nonplussed. "Um, what?" was all the reply she could muster.

He oozed cynicism as he explained, "You're barely an apprentice, but you've obviously had some training. But not here, and not at The Tower. So, who trained you, and what did they send you here for? Are you a spy for Lynod? A sneak-thief for Tianan? Who sent you?"

Draconic pride can only be pushed so far. Ariel stood to her full height, her eyes flashing to onyx pools, and her aura blasting contempt and disdain. The trolls paled, overwhelmed by the alien emotions she was projecting into them. The man, even shielded by his wizardrous power, shuddered under the onslaught.

Ariel gathered her will and pushed.

The wizard's shield buckled.

He fell back into his chair, sweat dripping from his expansive rolls of flesh, and tried to push back. He struggled and fought with every ounce of his trained will, grappling against the thrust of power Ariel smashed into his mind. She was by far the stronger! His wizardrous defenses, impervious to any sorcerer, crumbled like a castle of spun sugar caught in a tidal wave!

The trolls, caught in the edges of the conflict, howled in pain and rolled helplessly on the floor.

Suddenly, the wizard surrendered. "Please," he begged. "Please stop. I ... I didn't ... I ... please!" he stammered.

Ariel was moments away from tearing his last defenses to shreds. In seconds, she would own his heart and soul and he'd serve her as an abject slave if she wanted. But that wasn't what she wanted. It wasn't what her father would want her to do.

As abruptly as she had started the onslaught, she stopped. The wizard shuddered at the sudden relief. His bruised mind was mostly intact and still his own. He stared at Ariel in fear bordering on terror. Even had he been able to speak, his mind was too tumultuous to form thoughts that bore verbalizing.

The trolls, resilient as their kind always are, slowly stood up and shook off the shock and pain. But they stood at a respectful distance from Ariel and their postures spoke volumes about being unthreatening and docile. Deep instincts and keen senses finally made it clear to them that here was a predator beyond apex, stronger and more dangerous than they in every way imaginable.

Her voice cracking with anger and frustration, Ariel forcefully addressed the wizard. "My father sent me here to speak with your world's most powerful wizard. I'm told she only speaks with other master wizards, so I am here to be trained as a master wizard. You! Will! Help! Me!" Her eyes were pools of liquid black, metallic and filled with the emptiness and infinite power of the Void.

The wizard was too young to have ever met a dragon. He didn't know what had just happened. No sorcerer could assault a trained wizard that way. But if she herself were a wizard, she wouldn't have to fight him – she wouldn't even need to come to Xalax. Distance-speak was how wizards of that power communicated, not by walking through mountain passes and across the lands between. He was confused, and he did what any good bureaucrat would instinctively do when confused and overwhelmed. He passed the buck up the chain.

He didn't dare lower his defenses, useless though they might be, so he sent one of the trolls to carry a message to his master instead of distance-speaking him directly. The troll seemed relieved to be allowed to leave the room.

It took a few minutes for a master wizard to show up. Ariel was relieved that he was wearing something that looked more like clothing than like an assault on taste and aesthetics. He was handsome, looked like he might be in his thirties (she wasn't good at judging human age, and knew that wizards don't age the way mortals do, but she could assign a general decade of apparent age), and had a slight smile at the other wizard's discomfiture.

"My name is Sheppard," he led with. His manner asked the obvious question without words.

"Ariel," she replied, beginning to cool down. The swirling in her eyes slowed and calmed.

He continued, "I'm a master wizard. Journeyman Carnat asked me to speak with you regarding training in our school."

Ariel took a deep breath and calmed herself. Her eyes faded to a human appearance, with golden irises and round pupils.

"Master Sheppard, I am here to study to become a master wizard, so that I may speak with the Lady Magistrix about a task I have been set by my father."

"And your father is?" he asked.

Ariel looked sad for a moment. "Dead. My father is dead. He tasked me with speaking to the greatest wizard of this world, and sent me here for that. I must complete my errand, and I am prepared to learn to be a master wizard if that is what it takes."

Sheppard nodded agreement. "I'm sorry about your father. Carrying out his last wish is an honorable goal. I would like to help you, if you will come with me." He gestured for her to precede him out of the room.

They walked down several corridors and halls, across yards, and through two other buildings, and finally arrived in a large double-tower near the magical source at the base of the cliff. Even through the walls, she could feel the throb of power coming from that place. Here, so close, it was almost an actual noise or perhaps a tangible pressure. Before, she had only felt such power in the depths of the Void itself.

When they finally arrived at their destination, a room Sheppard had picked by means she did not know, it was a relief. The room was comfortable, with pleasant furnishings and only a modicum of decoration. It didn't distract her with appeals to draconic greed, nor did it offend her sense of taste and decorum. It was mostly decorated in earthy browns and dark green, and exuded warmth and calm.

Once they were seated, he spoke. "There are tests that must be taken before beginning an apprenticeship as a wizard. You already passed the first, when you correctly described 'stars' as other worlds, or shards of worlds. But that knowledge could be faked. A sorcerer could manipulate the tester's mind so he thought he had heard the correct answers, or could pluck the desired answers from the tester's own mind and repeat them back.

"You aren't a sorcerer, of course," he continued. "Despite your treatment of Carnat."

Ariel didn't want to interrupt, but she must have shown her curiosity on her face. He stopped and explained, "Sorcerers are men who can read men's minds and manipulate thoughts or emotions, even memories for powerful and skillful ones. They also have certain powers of scrying at a distance and such."

She thought a moment. "I agree that I'm not a sorcerer, but what makes you think it's obvious I'm not?"

He smiled mischievously. "I said 'men', and you aren't a man. *Men* who read minds and manipulate thoughts and emotions."

She smiled in spite of herself. His charm was winning her over. "Why are only men sorcerers?"

His eyes twinkled. "Because a woman who can read men's minds and manipulate their emotions and thoughts is simply a woman. There is no special word or category needed."

Ariel rolled her eyes. "I'm not sure…"

He interrupted her. "I'm pretty sure you can read my mind any time you want."

She looked at him and finally realized what his joke was. She nodded. "You're thinking about my tits, aren't you?"

His smile grew ear-to-ear and Ariel had to laugh as he nodded. "You see!" he exclaimed. "Women always know what men are thinking! And can always make men think about what they want."

"Okay," she conceded. "I can tell what men are thinking." His charm and humor made her feel safe, relaxed. She paused a moment and then continued, "You mentioned tests that would tell if I can actually become an apprentice wizard. What must I do? Make you think about something other than my breasts?"

He looked shocked. "Oh, no, no, no! Nothing so impossible as that. The tests would never be passed if they had to make a man think elsewise about you. No. Nothing like that. You simply have to judge some gemstones and tell me what value they have."

Ariel laughed musically, then sobered. "I'm no lapidariest, to judge the value of stones. Surely most of your apprentices aren't either. So, there is some trick to this that you don't wish me to know before your test. Shall we move on to the actual test? I like talking to you. You made me laugh, and that's rare these days. I appreciate it, but I really must become a master wizard as rapidly as possible."

Ariel was only being half-honest. As much as any dragon, she valued gems and precious metals, and, like most, she usually had a good idea of their value. But she was new to this world and this city, so she was honest insofar as she would not know the local worth of unfamiliar gemstones.

Sheppard nodded. "Okay then. To the test."

He pulled a small pouch out of a pocket in his shirt. "You see, I came prepared for this. The gems are in here. You must judge their value for me. Don't worry that you aren't trained to evaluate gemstones. That's the form of the test. The intent of the test is somewhat more wizardrous." He handed the pouch to her and settled back in his chair.

Ariel weighed the pouch in her hand. She could sense some slight magic inside it, but it was hard to gauge so close to that thrumming blast of power from the cliff.

With a final glance his way, she settled her attention on the bag. Perhaps there was something to it that was part of the test? If so, she could see nothing that was out of the ordinary about it.

After a brief examination, she decided it must actually be the contents that were the test, so she pulled the drawstring open and looked in.

There were three small gems inside. All were cut expertly. One was a small emerald, step-cut to a nicely formed rectangle about the size of a small pea. The second was a large diamond, about the size of her pinky fingernail, brilliant-cut in the usual round shape for such precious stones. The third was a blood-red ruby, rose-cut, intermediate in size between the other two. In the limited light inside the bag, she couldn't see much more detail than that, so she dumped them into the palm of her hand to look at them in better light.

The moment they touched her skin, she felt their magical presence push into her mind. Not an attack, like she'd done to Carnat, but a welcoming that contained almost-spoken words and clear thoughts.

She stared at them. To her eyes and her experience, the diamond was by far the most physically valuable. It would sell for much more than the others. Probably more than both together.

To her mind, the diamond spoke clearly of matters boring to her from long familiarity. The nature of the Void and how much power there was in it, the fact that life was the manifestation of the power of creation itself, the nature of worlds and how the gods had made them to house beings that were alive and possessed of free will. These were things her father had taught her before she could fly on her own wings and long-familiarity had distilled all fascination from them centuries ago.

The ruby seemed to speak of magical flames and power. Ways to bend the power of the Void to create elemental effects that mimicked the nature and power of spirits. The thoughts were strange and new, but they were clear and she felt she could, with time, understand them and even use the principles they were trying to teach her.

The emerald, however, was difficult. Somehow, it spoke of the basic nature of will itself. How the gods made the Void and how the human spirit cast a shadow in the Void and shaped it. It spoke to something deep in her – the key to her very nature as a dragon. And another key that she somehow knew made her also a wizard. It was difficult and the thoughts in it couldn't truly be turned into words or even solid concepts. There was something deeper about it. Something that went behind thought, behind existence even, and laid secrets bare that might destroy sanity like a gale blowing out a candle.

The emerald began to suck her mind and soul in. She could be lost in there! With a cry, she tossed the gems back into the pouch and pushed it back into Sheppard's hands.

Her eyes were wide and her face pale as she gathered her wits enough to ask, "What are those?"

He simply asked, "Which is the most valuable?"

Ariel had to spend a minute calming her racing mind and heart. The answer was overwhelmingly obvious, and it terrified her. "The emerald," she finally whispered.

Sheppard was shocked! His jaw dropped and he couldn't look away from Ariel's eyes.

He had to lick his lips nervously before he could speak. "The emerald?" he finally managed.

She nodded. She didn't trust herself to speak yet.

After a moment, he nodded. "Well, that definitely settles it. You're a wizard, certainly. And, if you don't kill yourself with uncontrolled or forbidden magic, you're bound to be a powerful one. No question about it after that."

He recovered from his shock and explained. "The gems are instruction stones. We have dozens of them, and they do most of the teaching of magic. The lore contained in them is in different grades.

"The diamond was imprinted with knowledge, in a fashion, for the instruction of apprentices. They study beginning lessons from it and either learn how to contact the Void and harness some amount of its power, or go insane from trying. Most of the people who fail this test think the diamond is the most valuable, because it would fetch the best price from a merchant in town. Only a wizard can sense the lessons and magic in it.

"The ruby contains more advanced lessons. Those who are actually ready to become apprentices can sense the lore in the diamond, but they sense the ruby is beyond them, and that the power it teaches is stronger, more advanced, more dangerous. They will value the diamond, but sense that the ruby is the more valuable stone to them. Beyond their current means to afford, but attainable.

"Most can't even sense the power in the emerald. Those who can, sense only the slightest presence of the mind that crafted it. Only the most gifted, those destined to become master wizards of great power, or die trying, can sense anything more from it than that.

"Truthfully, the emerald is beyond me, and I've been a master wizard for more than a century. The emerald is in the province of the Lady and her closest companions. The greatest wizards in the world study those gems. There are only six stones of that grade. Not all are emeralds, just as not all apprentice-stones are diamonds and not all journeyman stones are rubies.

"That you sensed power in the emerald is rare. That you sensed it was the most valuable, and sensed it strongly enough to know it is dangerous – I've never met anyone who could do that. I've never even heard of anyone who could do that.

"Who *are* you?" he concluded, wonderment in his eyes and manner.

"I am Ariel. And I wish to become a master wizard," she said. Her composure had recovered fully, while curiosity about the emerald burned bright inside her. "What's next?" she asked.

Chapter 5: Not "The Tower"

When the world was first created,
the titans on the work-crew crafted every
feature. Every hill and mountain, river,
lake, sea or stream, every rock, every
breath of wind – all this and more was
made by their labors, and known
intimately to them.

One thing, one thing alone, they
found, already in place before their
creation began. A tower, wondrous in size
and nature, was not by their skill made and
should not have been in their world, but
was. Of all the wonders of the world, it is
the oldest, and the only mystery to the
even the titans. None know from whence
it came. Its passages through the Void,

between two unrelated worlds, are unmatched in all of creation.

Unique unto the tower is its guardian, whom wizards call Sam for reasons even they cannot articulate.

It is not known who first found the tower, nor who first realized its potential as a place of magic. Druids lived there before wizards, and even they do not know whereof Sam came into being. The world-titan does not speak of her, and Sam herself gives no slightest clue to the mystery of her origin.

When the Lady Magistrix first sent wizards to the tower, to learn the deeper secrets that only those born for mastery can plumb without breaking their minds beyond insanity, they made many skillful efforts to scry Sam's origin, and that of the tower. Whereas the secrets of the Void reveal themselves perhaps too readily in that mystical place, the secrets of Sam and her tower remain inviolate against all attempts. – Official Histories of Xalax

Ariel sat at a desk next to Sheppard's bed, reading studious papers deep in the darkest part of the night. She had studied thus for many years, awake when all other were asleep, and her apprenticeship was much accelerated by this advantage.

Sheppard knew she studied late into the night, but he was not aware that she never once slept. Nor that she didn't burn candles or lamps to read in the dark. Wizard-light, easy to conjure, would have woken him up. Candle-light or lanterns might have, but it was never tested. To her eyes, even in her human form, the pages would have been as clear in the depths of an unlit mine as they were to a human in broad daylight.

If she had not been sworn to her father to never reveal her trueform, they would have been more clear yet, but she had not taken off her disguise since her arrival to this world, and would not remove it where there might be any witness.

She was a dragon, and had the patience of centuries, but she knew the threat of the gnomes was not going to await her convenience. Still, she had found no plan to approach the Lady Magistrix except by becoming a master wizard.

She did not know that dragons cannot be wizards. No one had ever told her. Thus she did not know that she had already done the impossible by becoming an advanced apprentice. Everyone assumed she could see the worlds in the Void because wizards can do so. Though Ariel knew she could see them because she was born a dragon, she did not know the significance of her dual-being.

When assumptions are not contradicted, they are not commonly questioned.

Ariel also had spent no time with the emerald that fascinated her. The other stones, and many like them, were becoming familiar to her. Even many of the journeyman stones, which took magic to a more active level of creation, were not unknown to her, despite her few years in the school. But she had been informed that that particular stone was only used in the apprenticeship test, and was otherwise held by the Lady herself and not available to others.

Sheppard, and a few of the other teachers, mostly advanced journeymen themselves or very junior masters, had kept her progress deliberately slow. Magic and wizardry are inherently dangerous, and the greatest danger is attempting power or knowledge beyond one's grasp. Even talent such as Ariel's, which came to the school only every four or five generations of man, had to be kept to a pace that was safe. Total mastery of apprentice materials was the only safeguard against the insanity lurking in more advanced studies.

So, sleepless as all of her kind always were, she studied into the night. Her nights were never interrupted after lovemaking with

Sheppard left him deeply asleep. She had quickly grown accustomed to his snoring and occasional sleep-talking and they did not interrupt her. She still remembered the first time she had heard him speak in his sleep, when she had tried to answer his questions. She had been first shocked by his nonsensical maunderings, then amused. Now, years later, she ignored them as the meaningless noises they were.

She heard someone approaching the door and recognized the heartbeat and breathing of one of the senior masters, a talented wizard named Jerome, with whom she had studied a few times. She wondered why he would be in Sheppard's tower at this odd hour of the night, and then realized he was actually coming right to their bedroom door.

By the time he got to the door, she was already easing it open. Jerome, fist raised to knock in a slightly comedic pose, stood there awkwardly for a moment. He had to swallow a few times and was having trouble gathering his composure enough to deliver whatever message he had arrived with. He kept trying to avert his eyes from Ariel's nude beauty, but couldn't quite manage to keep from staring.

She slipped past him into the hall and closed the door behind her, to keep any noise from disturbing Sheppard's sleep. This didn't seem to help Jerome's composure at all, but he finally got his eyes to lock over her left shoulder.

He tried to whisper, but his voice cracked briefly like a teenage boy's. "The Lady Magistrix has sent me to tell you that you are to depart immediately for Sam's Tower. You will leave at first light carrying only those things of your personal possession that you need for travel. You are to leave behind any of the gem-books that you are studying, since you won't need those at the tower, and we cannot risk allowing them to leave the bounds of the school."

He paused for thought, his eyes again distracted towards Ariel's breasts. Finally surrendering to human nature, he simply stared at her while he continued. "It's traditional to visit the temple and get the blessings of Kamaia and her sister before you leave the city. Their blessing will make the travel easier, at least for a few days. You will have to walk quite a long way, as journeymen are not allowed to use vehicles or mounts except those that are needful to cross water. If you have coin to pay for passage across the Great Eastern Ocean, I suggest you take it with you and save it for exactly that."

He paused and finally gathered his will again to look away. Before leaving, he managed to control his wayward voice just enough to suggest, "You should probably put on some clothing before you go."

Ariel didn't giggle at the bulge in the front of Jerome's pants. Human sexual behavior, she was convinced, was designed to get the minimum of pleasure and fun out of the maximum of embarrassment and discomfort. At these times, it was hard to imagine her own distant ancestors had once been human, and it was easy to understand why they had desired to transcend that and had become dragons instead.

She woke Sheppard up gently. He was still yawning and alternating between rubbing sleep out of his eyes and patting down his disheveled hair while she told him what the Lady's messenger had relayed to her. He had that "force my eyes open and I'll be awake" look when she asked, "He said I must walk, and that I should visit Kamaia's temple before leaving. I do not understand the connection. What does Kamaia's temple have to do with walking? I thought they were just a sort of sex-cult or something?"

Sheppard laugh-yawned. "And you certainly don't need help from the spirit-world in that department, do you?"

"I'm serious!" she said. "Do I really need to go there before I leave? I'm perfectly capable of walking without help. I walked here, didn't I?"

He smiled to smooth things over. "Of course you can walk. But visiting helps. And it would be taken amiss by the masters of the school if you skipped that part of the journey. There are those who already think you avoid too many of our traditions and ways. I argue that you weren't born to our life, but there is pressure in the Master's Council to limit your learning.

"They already don't want you to learn any war-magic, for fear you might use it against us. I point out that's nonsense, and the Lady seems to agree, but she hasn't overridden their injunction.

"Following the usual path, the traditional path, will help keep feathers from ruffling. Please, for our sake. Even though you can walk on your own and certainly don't need the temple's help in waking up your sexual prowess!"

Ariel had wondered why other apprentices were learning more self-defense than she was. Now it made sense.

She nodded and agreed, "As you say. I will start at the temple." It was important to earn these people's trust, as it was her only route to complete the task her father had set for her in those last desperate minutes before Dragonhome was destroyed utterly and her father with it.

Their farewell lovemaking occupied the rest of the night and had a poignancy and ardor to it that left both sated and relaxed.

After that, it took only a few minutes, and a few last sweet kisses, for her preparations to leave. Wearing light clothing and sturdy boots, carrying only a walking stick and a small pouch of Sheppard's money for the ocean passage, she left the school as soon as the false-dawn spread it's crepuscular light over the sky.

On the way out, she had the glad chance to say goodbye to Gregory, her troll friend, and then she passed through the school's gates out into the city for the first time in several years.

She paused on the threshold and looked back at the school. She had built memories there. Good ones of her time with Sheppard and Gregory. Interesting ones when she had witnessed, from afar, magical rituals of the leaders of the school. Though she had never met the Lady Magistrix in person, despite some attempts, she had seen her perform powerful wizardry as part of her education. She did not regret leaving, for it put her that much closer to completing her quest, but she did need a moment to gather herself and move on.

Seeing it, she could tell that the city hadn't changed much, but now she saw the patterns of creation in everything. The surge and ebb of the crowds, the dark-cloud passage of pigeons – their flocks so dense they blocked sight of the sky – the echoing of a thousand animal-noises from packs of dogs and squalling cats and a thousand other inhuman voices.

The city was the same, but every aspect of it had new meaning in her eyes, and it was wondrous to her in a way that no human dwelling ever had been before!

Wizardry, she had learned, was all about changing the patterns that creation wove into the substance of worlds. Power came from the Void, but it had no use without pattern. Before, she had seen the surfaces of things, or the strong auras of human emotion. Now she saw that every moment was created by the patterns of the prior moment that was destroyed, and set in turn the patterns of the next moment that would inherit reality.

All magic, all of the wizardry she was taught, came from the birth of patterns, the creation of each instant of Now. She felt that there was something more, something that the ancient emerald had hinted at, but the idea evaded her and slipped just beyond her grasp every time she reached for it.

She had grown accustomed to the patterns and moments of the school. Now she reveled in the city. So much life! So much color and shape and purpose! So many people drawing power from the Void to fuel their every intention and desire! It was awesome and amazing and she had to force herself to remember that she had a purpose herself, a goal of her own.

Resolutely, she set off towards the temple. "Each step, each moment, each tiny movement, leads to the next," she reminded herself. "Without purpose, all is chaos. With purpose, all is pattern. Only purpose grants pattern and meaning to creation. Only the living being can grant purpose, and only the trained being can control the patterns and purposes it creates." The earliest lessons of wizardry. She had never before thought the laws of magic would apply to something as simple as walking down streets to reach a destination!

"Magic is just living beyond the understanding of those who call it 'magic'. There is no difference between being alive and performing magic, except the perception of the form the creation and purpose take," another of the first lessons.

From these remembered lessons, she saw a glimpse of the reason for journeymanship, for being made to walk to Sam's tower. Even for not taking lessons with her – to force her to learn from life itself, where the lessons weren't thoughts impressed into gems by trained minds.

Thus occupied by the wonders of the living world, her walk to the temple was over before she was ready. She stood on the front steps to the large building and paused for one more look around before going inside.

The main building was quite large, almost half a mile on each side. It was only a couple of stories tall, and had no outside windows and only the one large entrance. The whole thing appeared to be made of basic stone – huge blocks of dark gray, without the fanciful carvings and paintings and decorations favored by the rest of the city and the school.

The steps up to the entrance ran the whole width of the front of the temple. Each step was several strides across and only a few inches high, but there were enough of them that the entrance was a dozen feet above the level of the street in front of it. The front of the building had rose vines growing all over it, with flowers in colors the rainbow would be jealous of, and the entrance was flanked by two large statues of a beautiful woman with emeralds for eyes, just as Gregory had described it to her.

Even this early in the day, with the sun just about to peek over the cliffs at the eastern edge of the city, there were hundreds of people passing in and out of the temple, and hundreds more gathered on the steps. Ariel's keen ears picked out each conversation of the many who were talking, and she quickly understood that most were there for healing of one sort or another, and most of the rest were concerned about children.

She saw dozens of pregnant women gathered on the steps. Many sat at hobbies or simple tasks, some gathered in groups and gossiped. Something in the temple reached out intangibly and affected their patterns and the patterns of their unborn children. It was magic, but not of the wizardly sort. Ariel decided it must be something Kamaia was doing, or perhaps her unnamed sister. She had heard of their connection to sex and reproduction, and now could sense it all around the temple. The magic was complex and too hard to follow, far beyond her comprehension, and it was beautiful in a way she had never seen before.

Ariel was met at the door by one of the priests. A handsome young man who smelled of absurdly good health and was wreathed in the odors of fertility and sex. She knew enough to realize that most human women would find him completely irresistible.

"Welcome to our temple, my lady," he said in a melodious voice. His eyes spoke of more than a simple welcome, but Ariel was accustomed to this from almost every man she'd ever met, and his lust made no impression on her. "How may we be of service to you this morning?"

From his words, odor and aura, Ariel knew how much he was hoping she was there to get pregnant. It was pretty obvious he would leap at the opportunity to help with that chore!

"I'm beginning a long journey, and I was instructed to seek out the blessing of the temple so I may travel well," she replied. His disappointment was tangible.

"Ah, well then, I shall take you to visit the priestess so you may commune with the Sisters," he replied. He gestured for her to walk into the inner temple, but she indicated she would follow him. He valiantly swallowed his disappointment she wouldn't walk ahead of him and let him ogle her from behind, and then led her deep into the massive building.

Ariel was surprised that his path led them down several flights of stairs. Humans usually preferred to be higher up, and the more important they thought they were, the higher they preferred to be. Either the priestesses weren't quite human (dwarves maybe?), or they were uncommonly humble, or there was something else going on that she hadn't caught up with yet.

Finally, they approached a huge set of solid bronze doors. Easily two stories high, and wide enough to allow a pair of ox carts to pass side-by-side, the doors were immensely solid and polished to a mirror-finish. They were guarded by a pair of huge trolls, but the doors looked far too massive for even trollish muscles to budge.

Ariel understood when the guards each took ahold of the door, and a surge of vitality and power came through the door and granted them superhuman strength.

The doors slid open easily, and Ariel's dragon-vision and wizard-senses were flooded with a rush of titanic energy! The solid bedrock-stone of the temple was morning-mist tenuous and ephemeral in the wash of Void-power flowing into the space beyond the door!

An inhumanly perfect, feminine voice came from within that cascade of power. "Come in, Void-Daughter, we must talk."

Ariel's eyes grew wide. Nobody here knew her true nature, but only the formal scholars of Dragonhome had ever called dragons "Void-Daughter" or "Void-Son". This was impossible!

Dragons can stare at the raw sun without blinking or harm, but Ariel's eyes were watering and she could only squint into the brightness-that-wasn't-light beyond the doors. Slowly, she made herself walk in. As she passed them, the guards silently closed the doors behind her.

She could barely feel the stone beneath her feet, and could see nothing but white brightness as she slowly stumbled forward. She couldn't tell how far she had passed before she caught sight of two perfect women standing ahead of her. They had the dark features of the local people, but sculpted into an elfin beauty that was both intensely human, and simultaneously surpassed even dragon-standards.

Both had heavy breasts, tipped with large, dark-brown nipples. Their hips were wide and well-shaped. Ariel had frequently seen the "glow" that healthy pregnant women get, and these two were filled with the purest version of that possible. They weren't themselves pregnant, but they were instead the very avatars of what it meant to be.

Where the local population had hazel or brown eyes, these two had eyes that glowed with a bright green vitality.

One was undecorated, but the other was covered head to toe in an incredibly beautiful and detailed tattoo of a rose-bush in full bloom.

They spoke in chorus, their two voices perfectly synchronized into a single sound. "Void-Daughter, our Lord spoke to us of your coming. He tells us that we must keep your secret, and that you have little time left for your quest. The gnomes approach our world, and will arrive in only a few handfuls of years. He says you must travel, but not to the tower of his favorite creation. Instead, you must go to the land where only the dead prosper. You will find the help we need there. Our world's only hope lies with the one who is the master of his own death.

"You have been unintentionally mislead about the goal of your father's quest. The Lady of the school is not and never has been the most potent wizard in this world. Your father did not send you for her.

"You will cross the wide ocean. But then you must go south, not east. You will know when you find the lands ruled by the death that isn't dead.

"There, you must learn wizardry from the only master who can bring you to your full gift. Void-Daughter, you must become the mistress of the very Void itself. Only one can help you in that journey. He waits, and knows of your approach.

"Void-Children, born of wizardry and the might of our lord's brothers and sisters, cannot be wizards, but you are exempted from this law by power beyond that of our Lord.

"Do not expect to be greeted warmly. You must persuade the dead master to teach you, and he will not be won over easily. He has no love for the wizards of this world, though he does not reflect their hatred. You must not try to dragon-charm or manipulate or trick him. He is immune to such things, and will despise you if you are not honorable with him.

"Our Lord cannot tell you more than that, for he does not know the future, only the moment and the patterns of the past. He can influence much, but the ruler of the dead is no subject of our world nor anything of it."

Sudden pain washed over Ariel's back! She doubled over and fell to the floor, helpless in agony.

"Our Lord heals you, as only he can," the priestesses combined voices sang through her haze of anguish. The skin on her back moved like a thing alive on its own, and the pain of her scars, where gnomish weapons had raked her flesh, flooded her every sense.

There was a flash, too intense for even dragon-eyes, and Ariel found herself standing in the hallway, the doors closed behind her. The young priest, with lust still in his voice, asked, "You have received the blessing of the priestesses and the Sisters. Are you finished with your need in our holy place?" The guards stood like statues.

The pain was gone. The doors were just doors. No world-shaping power lurked behind them. Ariel knew she had met the world-titan, the master-craftsman who had not only built the world she stood upon, but in some very real sense *was* the world. But he was gone now. The priestesses would be priestesses – possessed by some of the most powerful healing and fertility spirits in the world, but human once again. She knew she was done here, her errand complete, and it was time to leave.

She turned and walked out of the temple. She didn't notice or care that the priest followed her out to the door and that his eyes never went above her waist-line for the whole distance. Her mission, her real mission, not this side-trip to the tower, demanded her attention and thought.

The whole way out of the city, Ariel barely looked at her surroundings. Her eyes and feet kept her on auto-pilot and carried her to the northern gate. From there, she could follow the road till it curved east, around the plateau-lands the city abutted against. It was an easy path, and would present no dangers she could not easily master, but it was a long one, and the titan had told her time was running short.

She made her decision and started running.

Faster than any human, faster even than an elf, she sprinted down the road. She needed to get away from the city before she could take on her true-form. Far enough away that none would see her transformation. The people of this world must not know of her true nature, and she felt a need for speed beyond what a human body could achieve.

Minutes and miles passed quickly. As was the nature of dragonkind, she did not grow tired or hot or uncomfortable from the flat-out sprint. When she judged she was far enough away from the city that no prying eyes would see her transformation, she braced herself for the pain she expected, and willed away the illusion of human-form she had worn for all these years.

In the death of Dragonhome, gnomish weapons had burned off her beautiful wings, leaving only horrible scars on her back. That they had meant to kill her and steal her living essence and had failed did little to comfort her for the loss and the pain. Every moment in her true-form had been a paean to agony ever since.

She winced before she willed the transformation, anticipating the shock of agony.

Like a man who pushes harder than he needs to against a door that another is opening from the other side, she braced herself for what wasn't there!

No pain!

No torn and burned flesh!

The titan had healed her and returned her glorious wings!

Air swept under them as she leapt, joyous, into the air! She had not felt flight in decades, and the revel of it flooded through her as she threw herself into the realm of wind and left the ground racing away below her!

Better than sex!

Better even than laughing!

She swooped and soared and bellowed her rapture to the spirits of storm and wind that raced with her!

Far away, she could see the ocean and the land beyond it. Something marred the view beyond the far edge of the wide water, and she knew that was where she must go.

With joy in her heart and a dance in her wings, the last dragon swept over the land far beneath her. Walking, even running, would take days to cross the land and sea. Flying on dragon wings, it would be done before it was time for breakfast.

She flew towards the rising sun, but was careful not to leave the realm of the world below her. If she flew too high, into the raw Void, she could fly far, far faster than in the realm of a world. She could outfly the light of the sun if she wanted to leave this shard behind, but coming back to the world from the Void was tricky, and she could end up years delayed and thousands of miles off-course. It took special magic to enter a world, and it was capricious even at the best of times. Far better to fly slower, stay in the realm of the world-shard, and get to her destination in a few short hours.

The pure joy of flight had always been her greatest pleasure, and she had thought it lost forever. She felt reborn in the joyous revel of being whole!

Even the seriousness of her quest and the mysteriousness of her destination couldn't keep the young dragon from breaking into dance in the high air. It had been too long since she swooped and swirled and looped and dove and banked like only a dragon can.

For the first time in decades, Ariel truly smiled.

Chapter 6: On Strange Shores

When foul gnomes, abomination of
the created world-shards, threatened her
own world, the Lady sent Ariel to beg
intervention from the very god Death.
In eternal darkness, surrounded by
a black land of poison and bereft of all life,

hope or love, Death ruled his court of dark things.

> *Vampires, lords of the night and mist, spawned plans of bloodlust under Death's cruel reign.*
>
> *Wraiths, bodiless incarnations of fear and hopelessness, writhed in the shadows of that land.*
>
> *Death's bodyguard, dozens of the skeletal remains of soldiers punished with unlife for betrayals too twisted for the human mind to comprehend, surrounded him.*
>
> *His creations were dreadful to behold, corrupt and hideous, but Death himself was deceptively beautiful. His hateful power and lies and were clothed in inhuman glory, the better to tempt those who lusted for immortality and forbidden knowledge.*
>
> *To this cursed kingdom, the Lady sent Ariel, for no mortal, nor even a wizard, could safely travel those poisoned lands, but the Lady knew the last dragon could safely tread where others would perish. – <u>the official histories of Xalax</u>*

The molten sun blazed down on parched earth all through the wide valley. Soil bleached by centuries in an unrelenting solar furnace blended with salt left when ancient seas evaporated, leaving behind a mix of light tan and gray-white that shimmered the air above it.

It was a mild summer afternoon, which meant 130 degrees in the shade, if there had been any, and ground almost hot enough to boil water. Living things, long adapted to the heat and blinding glare of sun and salt, buried themselves in the dirt and sand, or hid in caves or under rocks. Nothing moved in the afternoon except the furnace-winds and the fine dust they deviled into hundreds of gyres.

In the deepest part of the valley, where the ground was dry as a kiln even though it was hundreds of feet below sea level, a fortress was being built. Day and night, through hottest summer days and winter nights cold enough to freeze, thousands of workers tirelessly built ramparts of adobe and massive sandstone blocks. Towers clawed hundreds of feet into the sky and stygian tunnels bored miles deep into the bedrock below.

The outer walls, over a hundred feet high and dozens of yards thick, were constantly being mended, from the sandstorms and heat-damage, reinforced, and added to, and had been for centuries, day in and day out. Hundreds-of-thousands of workers, more tireless than ants and more driven, continuously creating the greatest defensive bulwark in all the world.

The workers ignored equally the hot sun, the waterless waste, the blazing light and the darkest depths of the tunnels. Tunnels filled with water or poison gasses bothered them not at all. For the workers were all long-since dead, and needed not the things of life. They broke no fast, drank no fluid, breathed no air. Most had no eyes to blink and no skin to burn in the unfettered sunlight, for they had no living flesh at all, just bone and leathery ligaments, magically reinforced and reanimated as a horrid mockery of life.

Inside the citadel, in fortified towers and monstrous edifices with thick walls and only a few arrow-slits for windows, millions more of the undead trained endlessly in the arts of war.

One day, their master would unleash them on his enemies, and they longed for that opportunity. Hunger, lust, exhaustion, they knew not. The passion for slaying was their whole world, and they were complete with only that.

In the highest rooms of a massive tower, almost ten-thousand feet above the desert floor, the lord and master of the citadel sat on a throne made entirely of a metal unnamed and unknown to man or wizard. His thoughts roamed the world, unconfined by his long-dead body, influencing a decision here, twisting a plan there, eternally preparing for apocalyptic war.

Black leather that had once been skin stretched tight over his skeletal body, as dry and unyielding as the salt-pans outside his city. His corpse was cased in unworldly platemail armor of alien metal that glimmered all the colors that his flesh denied. Thousands of runes and sigils covered the armor's every surface. At his side rested a monstrous sword, glimmering brighter than silver and richer than gold, carved with runes of ancient power and embedded with bright gems that glittered a thousand rainbow-hues in the faint light he allowed in his harsh throne room. Gemlike light gleamed pale, purest sapphire-blue in his otherwise empty eye sockets, shedding just enough light to emphasize the absolute black of his horrifying face.

He was alone, so none noted the sudden flare in the blue glow where his eyes should have been as his attention flashed across the sea. A messenger was coming to him! For the first time in a century, he stirred in his throne, the faintest motion in his ancient, mummified flesh.

All through the citadel, the walking dead felt their master's sudden interest. A ripple of anticipation washed over the countless undead. Soon, they knew. It would be soon.

***

Ariel was close to the shore of the continent that was her destination. This close, she could see that there was a definite area that was somehow shrouded from her vision. Dragon-sight can penetrate vast distances, and see through mist, or even liquid water, almost as well as through clear air, but there appeared to be a fog, proof against even her eyes, over a wide region.

North of the obscured area was a vast desert with patches of green, scattered rivers and canyons, and some arid mountain ranges breaking it up. South of the area was more desert, and a narrow sea that jutted inland from the south in almost a straight line. Further south was a narrowing strip of land that eventually joined another continent that spanned the solar-midline of the world. She could see large mountains on the near side of that continent, but wasn't high enough to see over them to the east. Another high mountain chain was the limit of her vision over the northern continent. She knew, from her studies there were lands beyond it, but she couldn't see them from her vantage over the ocean.

She knew Sam's Tower was far to the east beyond those mountains, but she had no line of sight to it unless she rose so high she might accidentally escape the world and have to take time to re-enter it.

To the furthest north, she could see a winter-land and icy seas. Many mountains blocked her view that way, and the land was rippled and crumpled in the way that told her volcanoes and earthquakes would be common along the edge, where earth fought with earth, egged on by the deep fires of the world-shard. This was common to many worlds and she had seen it many times before.

Some dragons she had known, before the gnomes had slain them all, had told her tales of digging deep into worlds and passing through the realm of pure-earth to the fused realms below where earth and fire melded and made the living foundations of the worlds. She had never ventured there herself, but she knew it was a realm of pressure and heat, where solid metal and rock were fluid and fire was solid and liquid at the same time.

She was bored after flying this far, and stray thoughts on the shape of this world-shard and the realms she had never visited bubbled through her mind. Dragons were born to explore strange new worlds and go where men couldn't, and ever their attention wandered to such things and such places.

On the shore near her, she could see several villages and towns of humans, and even a colony of elves. The elves were too far north, away from the obscured area. While they might know about it – elves often possessing wisdom about many things – she knew her appearance there would be more likely to cause grief and anger than to gain anything useful. Elves envied many things – dwarves for their riches, wizards for their power, even other elves –

but they envied dragons over all others. Flying there would just tempt them to their petty spites and hateful games.

There were several human villages much closer to the boundary of the mist-that-wasn't-mist. Some even right at the edge of it. She decided that one of these would be the best place to learn something of what was beyond that barrier, and directed her flight to the largest of them.

The village appeared prosperous to her. It had substantial farms and ranches around it, numerous buildings, and had the fortified forms that humans use to protect their wealth and their lives from others of their own kind.

A very durable-looking wall ringed the main body of the village, and all of the buildings inside that perimeter had windowless ground-floors and iron bars over the wide windows they kept above that level. The walls and buildings had none of the battlements and crenellations that she had grown accustomed to in Xalax, but they were very solidly made of stone and brick, and well-reinforced with flying buttresses and heavy timbers.

The farm-houses in the lands nearby were all miniature fortresses, with well-made walls, enclosed and gated courtyards, and bars over windows and doors.

Even from a distance, she could see that all the doors had silver-inlaid writings or decorations, and were striped with bars of wrought iron. It was a strange form of decoration, with no function she could perceive, but she knew human tastes varied far more than those of dragons, and she initially took no meaning from it.

The iron bars on all of the windows also all seemed to be decorated with silver, or wrapped in strips of silver-wire. No copper, no brass, no bronze nor gold, just iron and silver everywhere.

When she was close enough to see with wizard-sight, she perceived that all of these things, the walls, the iron bars, the silver markings and wires, were all imbued with magical barriers. Someone was spending a tremendous amount of magical power to protect this village! Against what, she could not tell, but she suspected it had something to do with the opaque mist that roiled just outside the eastern wall.

She landed far enough away that nobody would see her trueform, and put on her illusion of humanity. In keeping with the fashion she had seen on women in the village, she dressed in a simple toga of many-colored cotton. The pattern she chose was tie-dyed in hues of rose and pale blue and dozens of shades of yellow and green. The garment draped over one shoulder, covered most of the torso, including her breasts, and hung a few inches past the hips and groin, covering only a small part of her upper legs. The women she had seen were bare from there down, so she too wore no shoes nor anything else below that line.

She could not see, from the air, if they wore anything beneath the toga, so she was bare beneath as well, but it was covered by the opaque cloth from most eyes, unless she should sit or bend over at the waist.

Her skin she chose to have as a golden tan, smooth and perfect in tone and texture. Her hair she kept long, and in her usual pale blue with lavender tips and highlights. Her eyes were golden-irised and glittered in the bright sunlight.

By instinct that never failed, she knew the men of this place would be most pleased by large breasts, so she formed them so, and made her hips wide and round below a narrow waist and flat stomach with a hint of muscle rippling beneath the smooth skin and shapely navel.

She did not want to hurry, but preferred to take her time approaching the village. She needed to observe. To look and listen. To taste the dust and air, to smell the distant scents of a mass of humanity. The farms she walked past revealed much in their odors, the flavor of the dirt, the taste of droplets of moisture in the air around them. The road she walked on, a well-traveled dirt path, passed on a library of knowledge about the village and those who traveled to and from it. She needed these things, not just because dragons enjoy meeting people and learning about them, but because she needed to make allies of these people so she could learn of the lands beyond them.

In distant Xalax, it was still early in the day, such was the speed of her flight, but here, thousands of miles to the east, it was nearly suppertime.

When she met up with other travelers on the road, they were friendly and polite beyond what she was accustomed to. Her beauty and grace usually garnered some level of approachability in most humans, but these people seemed to go above and beyond in their manners and friendliness with each other and with her.

She also noted that not one wore or carried any sort of weapon. No swords, no spears, not even a sharp knife! In preparation for supper, they carefully stored their tools and farming implements and did not carry them around.

Halfway to the village, she was met by farmers carrying goods in a wagon pulled by the largest dogs Ariel had ever seen – the size of small horses, with broad chests and powerful legs. Four of them pulled the large wagon easily. The farmers invited her to join them in the wagon, and she was grateful for the ride. Not because she would tire from walking, but because it was novel to ride behind canine beasts of burden, and because she wanted to converse with the farmers.

The farmers introduced themselves as Madro and Der, and indicated they were brothers-in-law. They had copper-colored skin, a sort of red-brown, long black hair on their heads and no facial hair at all. Both were strongly built and had the callouses of hard work and skin that spoke of long hours in the sun and wind.

From them, she learned the village was named The Place of Angels, in the local language. She asked what "angels" were, and learned that they were the holy assistants of the gods. She asked if they meant titans, but the men shook their heads no and tried to explain that angels don't build worlds, they carry messages and do errands for the gods, while titans are the craftsmen of the void. She'd never heard of angels before, so could neither gainsay nor confirm the idea. It idea intrigued her idle curiosity, but she had much more on her mind and soon dismissed the idea as unimportant to her current errand.

The city was the industrial center of a large and complex nation of small towns, large farms, and many wandering merchants and migrant workers. People from thousands of miles to the north and south came here to trade, usually bringing raw materials and taking away finished goods of the sorts that semi-independent farms could not make or repair on their own.

She was told that all the best iron workers and silversmiths lived in Angeltown, as she began to think of it. Whenever a new building was needed, she learned that the silver-and-iron screens necessary to ward the windows were all made here, along with the silver stars and wards needed to properly secure doors.

The farmers knew she was from far away, because she did not know these things about doors and windows. "You must be indoors, protected by silver and iron, at night," they advised her. "It is not safe to be out in the dark. Dangerous things lurk around once the sun is down."

When she asked about the not-mist east of the village, they did not know what she meant. To their eyes, east of the village was just the edge of the desert, and then the mountains. When Ariel used only human senses, she could see the things they spoke of. But dragon-sight and wizard-perceptions both went no further than the east wall of the village. Even the patterns of creation seemed to end there, which was impossible.

"I do not know this mist you are asking about, but I do know that nobody goes east of here. No roads, no paths, nowhere to go. Only the dead go east, and we do not hurry to join them," Madro, told her.

Der, added, "Maybe the dead see this mist you see. Maybe you were drawn to our village the way they are drawn into the desert." He looked sad, but would answer no further questions on that subject.

Ariel was familiar with many cultures from many worlds, and so very many of them had stories of lands of the dead, or pathways the dead travelled, or any number of other explanations for death. She assumed this was simply the local flavor of that common dish.

As they approached the village, people were gathering to eat and the whole place smelled of stew and beans and dozens of spices and herbs.

Ariel found that, in preparation for dinner, children were spreading bunches of flowers over the doorsteps and porches of the buildings, adding a sweet layer to the aromas.

She was pleased to note that they had no open sewers, and that the wells smelled of clean water. They were conscientious about hygiene in every way, and those who weren't preparing food were busy bathing with soap and warm water. Such attention to health wasn't necessary for her, but for humans she knew it was an important barrier against myriad diseases. So few humans paid attention to such details that she was surprised at how universal it seemed with these people.

They arrived to the village before the sun set, so people were still out and about in large numbers. Some stopped and stared at Ariel, but most were sufficiently accustomed to strangers traveling through that they ignored her as they would any other traveler.

Madro had invited her to stay the night in the inn that they favored, and she understood it was an invitation to his bed. He wasn't a handsome man, but she felt it would be impolite to refuse him after he had been so generous with his wagon, so she agreed.

She didn't bother renting a room of her own. Even if the farmer turned disagreeable, she felt she could safely escape and sleep on her own anywhere she liked. Humans might find danger in the dark, but she very much doubted any night-prowler of this world would threaten her in any meaningful way. Most predatory animals were savvy enough to avoid dragons, and those that weren't generally ended up as a light snack.

The three of them were standing on the porch of the inn, chatting with the innkeeper about the benefits of good food and cheerful company. Across the street, two men were repairing the bars on a third-floor window. One man was up the ladder, the other on the ground steadying it and passing tools and materials up to his companion. Ariel was paying more attention to her companions than to the tradesmen, so she almost didn't see what happened. A small dog, chasing an even smaller dog, raced around the corner of the building and bumped the man at the bottom of the ladder. The ladder toppled, and the man on it fell hard on the packed earth of the road. Ariel heard the snap as his neck broke.

Wizards can always tell when someone dies. They had no need to check for mist on a mirror or to press against arteries and feel for a pulse. At death, a person stops making patterns and intentions, and becomes part of the pattern instead. Any living thing, to an extent great or minute, puts patterns into reality. Only inanimate things do not, and this man was no longer making patterns. His body flailed wildly, nerves and muscles wrenching him to and fro, but it was the spastic movements of a dying body that no longer held a living soul. He moved, but was no more alive than a stream or a falling rock.

Everyone in sight froze in panic.

Women screamed.

Men shouted.

And then everyone was running! Pell-mell, they mobbed into doorways and trampled everything in their way!

A young woman struggled to race to a small child who stood crying in the middle of the street, while a man, perhaps her husband, wrestled her into a doorway. The moment she was held inside by others, he raced back into the street.

From half a block away, Ariel could hear his heart rushing in panic and could see the horror in his eyes.

But she could see nothing to fear!

Then the fallen body stirred.

Ariel realized she was alone on the porch. She had ignored the attempts of others to drag her inside, and now she heard the lock and bar secure the door behind her.

There were only four left on the street: the dead man, the father, the child, and Ariel.

The dead man suddenly stood. His motions were jerky and unbalanced, and she saw no mind behind his eyes. No human aura of emotion and semi-conscious thought radiated from him.

He was dead. No beat from his heart, no air moved in his lungs. But he stood and glared around.

The father was halfway to the building, desperately carrying his tiny child, when the dead thing's eyes swung his way.

Hellfire filled its eyes and it moaned as it leapt into pursuit!

Ariel roared! The porch shuddered under her suddenly titanic weight, and a jet of blue-green dragonfire sprayed destruction at the racing form of the dead thing!

The dragon watched in horror as the flaming monster ran past her and assaulted the man and child! It tried to tear into them with teeth and nails, but it was too burned and it merely slammed them to the ground.

But the fire spread!

Ariel's instinctive attack was turned against the very people she had tried to save, and the man and child rolled on the ground and screamed in utmost agony as the toxic, flaming corrosive burned into them.

In moments, the two were dead.

The thing that had attacked them immediately lost interest. All that was left of it was a smoking partial skeleton, whole areas of bone burned away along with the flesh her dragonfire had destroyed. But still it moved.

One last look around found no more human targets, only the giant dragon. Mindlessly, the thing began to crawl to the east, on stumps of its legs and half an arm.

As it moved, the father and child, badly burned, definitely dead, but still mostly intact, shuffled to their feet.

Ariel, mesmerized by horror, stared at them as they looked around, moaned, and started limping towards the east wall.

She could hear thousands of terrified human hearts gathered behind shuttered, barred windows and locked doors.

Some muttered prayers to various gods or spirits. Some cried. Some were locked in silence by terror and shock.

She could hear the howling wail of the woman who had first tried to rescue the child.

The three dead people moved steadily to the east wall and passed through an open gate. As they entered the mist, they lost the mindless death in their eyes and the dead father and daughter loped off into the desert, their postures and movements clean and filled with purpose and determination.

When the crawling, dragging ruin of the first man finally moved into the mist, he seemed to gain energy from somewhere, and his horrible movements became faster and smoother.

Ariel knew she would have to follow them into the east, and for only the second time in her long life, she felt terror. What was that place? And how had it done this terrible thing to these innocent people?

Magic could not break the laws of life and death! It couldn't! She had been taught that over and over. That was why even wizards and dragons could be killed. Of course a skilled wizard could animate a dead body, in the same way one could move rocks around or levitate water. But that was emphatically not what she had just witnessed! Those dead people had consciousness, had intentions, made patterns! Those things were the very definition of life. So they were dead and alive at the same time, and her whole mind could react only with horror at that terrible mix.

Had she been anyone else, she would have paused. Anyone else would have stopped, questioned the natives, made plans, gathered supplies, perhaps sent messages back to the school in Xalax to request advice or at least agreement with the necessity of going into that mist. But she wasn't anyone else. She was Ariel, the only dragon-wizard in existence, and she followed her instincts and curiosity without hesitation.

Her heart pounded in fear. Her mouth was dry and her hands were wet. But she knew the difference between feeling fear and being a coward, and she moved forwards towards the fear.

It took only moments to reach the gate, and she looked through it into the mist and the lands within it. To mortal eyes, they looked much the same as the lands in all other directions from the village. Dry hills covered in the kinds of plants that thrive where surface-water is scarce. Palms, oaks, dark-green shrubs, even some hardy grass in patches, gave a green haze over tan, sun-bleached dirt. In the distance, she could see snow-peaked mountains rising above the hills, but not above the mist.

The undead villagers had disappeared into the hills, but their tracks were easy to see and all pointed straight into the desert, towards the mountains in the north-east. Even the burnt one that was dragging itself was gone, but it left the easiest tracks of all.

Ariel looked around, taking in every detail she could, and then stepped into the mist and walked the path of the dead.

As soon as she stepped into it, she knew something was horribly wrong. Weakness washed over her muscles as her eyes blurred and her ears went deaf.

She could barely see! Colors were washed out, everything was dull. The whole world was devoid of detail and depth and character!

She could barely hear her own walking, and the light breeze that played over the land and hills. Accustomed to being able to count the heartbeats in the village behind her, and pinpoint the ones that were closest to doors or windows, the empty silence filled her with dread.

She almost stopped, but determination and courage again won out. Step after step, she moved deeper into the mist-lands.

As she walked, a strange sensation filled her body. It started in her legs as a dull pain she'd never felt before, and then spread upwards. Slowly, insidiously, as miles passed, she ached.

Sweat spread over her skin. She had never felt heat or tiredness before and it was horrible!

As she walked, the sun set, and the breeze cooled rapidly. She shivered for the first time in her life and felt the chill on her skin of cold night air.

Hours passed and she kept walking.

The pain increased and finally overwhelmed her. She was healthy and athletic, but she had been immune to exhaustion all her life, and it was torture!

By the time she stopped, she was cold and exhausted, her muscles were cramped, her feet were in agony, and her mind was dull and overloaded with new and horrible sensations.

Another sensation began crushing even her firm will. She had no name for it. It made her mind turn into cottony fog, it forced her eyes closed against her will, it sent her stumbling and left her disoriented and dizzy.

Ariel had never been tired before. She was the last of the dragons, and the first to ever need to sleep.

For a while, she trekked on, blindly forcing one foot in front of the other, stumbling over every step.

One stumble turned into a fall. Her body hit the ground, the dull, colorless, dirt that she could barely see in the dark. She blinked and tried to stand up. The blink went on and on and she was paralyzed and heavy and could not stand.

Her mind rallied one last time, and tried to force her pained body into trueform. But the call to remove the illusion and revert to being a dragon fell on numb nerves and drained will and no transformation took her away from her newly-mortal weakness.

She dreamed. The first dreams of the first sleeping dragon. Something was calling to her from deep in the desert. Something spoke to her from across the world. It said only one thing, over and over. Her father's secret, true-name.

Unbearable light forced its way through her thin eyelids and dragged her awake.

She looked around, only dimly aware of where she was. She knew where she needed to go, but it hurt so much to walk!

But walk she did.

More new sensations tore at her. Real hunger, the kind that must be filled for muscles to work was new to her, but it was quickly submerged in a more dire and urgent need for water.

The land was already hot when she awoke, and the sun baked her skin dry. Dust settled on her and turned briefly to mud in her sweat, but she was out of sweat soon enough and the dust sucked moisture from deeper inside her flesh.

It coated her skin. Her hair was dull gray by the time the sun peaked for the day. She stopped rubbing the dirt out of her eyes when her hands were dusty enough to make it worse instead of better.

Ariel had never learned the skills needed for survival in any terrain. Dragons did not need them. Any mortal would have fared better than she did, with less effort and better grace.

She did not seek shade, not knowing it would help.

She did not conserve her strength in any way.

She didn't even shade her eyes, and was soon enough blind from sunlight and dust.

Dirt settled into her nose, and she did nothing to prevent it for she did not know it could be done nor that it should.

As her nose dried out, she found she was panting through her mouth, and that too quickly became coated inside and out with fine sand and dirt.

Her fair skin burned deeply red and was quickly rubbed raw by the collar and seams of her light clothing.

Many of these things would have been easy to avoid or mitigate with any modicum of experience. Magic had always provided her every need, but, here, in this horrid place, she could summon nothing of the immense power of the Void.

A world without magic was impossible, a small voice in her exhausted mind kept telling her. No world-shard could exist without drawing its existence from the Void. This was all impossible! But no faintest hint of power answered her calls to it.

And soon those calls fell further and further apart.

She did not know she was dying, but she could feel it. She had no names for the sensations she was feeling. "Thirst" was a word to her, and she had a semi-grasp of what a human would mean by it, but she did not connect that word to how she felt. The same for "hunger" and "exhaustion".

All she knew was that it hurt. Every bit of her hurt. *That* she could put a name to! She knew pain well!

She wasn't aware that she had fallen.

She didn't know that she was lying on the ground, unmoving.

She did not notice darkness filling her mind.

***

Ariel started awake!

Her eyes flew open, and found no change in the darkness from being shut.

She felt cool, but not cold. And all the pain was gone.

Her eyes roamed the darkness, and found two points of pale-blue light were hovering a few feet to her left.

She realized she was lying on some hard, cool surface. Maybe stone, but she wasn't sure. Even now, her sense of touch was numbed nearly to uselessness.

She was nude, but felt no shock at that. She had never suffered modesty, and nakedness and helplessness were not equivalent in her experience.

There was moisture in her mouth, and she was breathing easily. After a moment, she decided to attempt speech.

"Hello?" she ventured. Her voice was a hesitant croak, but it worked. She instinctively worked muscles in her throat and the back of her mouth, loosening up her voice in preparation for a second attempt.

A rasp came from the direction of the sparks. It was hardly a voice, but it sounded like maybe it had once been one. "Hello, Ariel. Welcome to the Deadlands," it said.

Without prompting, it spoke again. "My name is Gem, and I am your host as you are my guest."

She thought a moment. "Am I dead, then?"

"No," he replied. "But you nearly were. My people rescued you from the edges of the desert and brought you to me. I healed your hurts and filled your flesh with water.

"It has been ages since I worked on a living body, and I am out of practice. So please forgive me if I have left any lingering discomfort."

Ariel took stock of her body and the still-dull sensations of it. "I think I'm hungry. If this is what humans call 'hunger.' It seems like it must be."

Gem said nothing, but Ariel felt he had heard her and was doing something about it.

Miles away, in the desert, one of the undead set down the rock-working tools it had been wielding and, at the silent command of its distant master, went out to hunt down some rabbits or coyotes. Its master wanted the flesh, uncorrupted and fresh, even still alive if possible. The skeletal figure had not hunted since its living days, centuries past, but it was intelligent enough to start figuring out how it would go about this task, and promptly got to work.

A few seconds had passed when Gem spoke again. "Food is being brought. I had forgotten about it. My apologies. It will be here in a few hours. I hope that will be adequate."

Ariel, still supine on what she realized must be a stone floor, shrugged. "I don't know hunger, not really, not as mortals do. But I'm certain I can last a few hours if I must. What option is there, else?"

The rasp chuckled – the sound almost more of a cough than a laugh. "True. Very true."

He paused, then, "I think I like you, young Void-Daughter. I liked your father, and I think I like you. You see things as they are, not as you wish they were or as you think they ought to be. And you made me laugh for the first time in a long while. Yes, I think I like you."

As he spoke, mage-light filled the air above them. Diffuse, pale, slightly blue-green, but more than enough for Ariel's dark-adjusted eyes.

She looked at him.

Any other would have screamed in terror.

Any other would have cowered from his black, leathery, mummified face.

Any other would have shrunk and tried to hide from the gem-fire where his eyes should have been.

But Ariel was not any other. She looked at him calmly. She appraised him as best her crippled sight allowed.

Finally, after gazing at him for a minute, she spoke again. "You named yourself Gem, but I do not know who you are?" Her voice made it a question, and her intent made it a wizardly one.

He could not really smile, for his lips had long since rotted away and left behind only exposed teeth, but Ariel would have sworn she could sense a smirk on his face.

"I am Gem. That is my true-name. It gives you no power over me and no defense from me. But what you really need to know, Ariel-of-many-natures, is that I'm your new teacher. I will teach you the truth about magic, and you will become an actual wizard.

"You are a dragon, and it is impossible for a dragon to be a wizard or for a wizard to become a dragon, but you are both despite all that. I see the handiwork of the gods in that fact.

"Your father trained you well and you are an excellent dragon, but you need real training to become a real wizard.

"Not one of those half-apprentices that call themselves 'masters' in old, worn-out Xalax. Not one of the cowardly hedge-mages that half-instruct false journeymen at Sam's hive. The real thing. The first new wizard on this world in a thousand years."

Ariel had expected getting him to teach her would take more work. The Titan had led her to believe it would take an effort to win Gem's trust and aid. She was, however, wise enough not to say so.

Instead, she replied tentatively, her voice more question than assertion. "I've seen the master-wizards in Xalax rain magefire on their enemies, and turn men into trolls. I've seen the Lady Magistrix transform soldiers into battle-mages who seem formidable by human standards. They seem wizardly to me," she said. She did not wish to offend him, but she felt that maybe he had not seen Xalax recently and was mistaken about it.

"Trolls?" he sneered. "Battle-mages? Playthings! You will meet my champions, both my ancient companions and my new ones, and you will judge for yourself what 'wizard' truly means!" His voice had no more expression in it than before, but, again, Ariel felt she could discern something of his mood by some means. She couldn't see his aura, if he even had one (only the living have auras and she was certain he was not that), but it was something similar.

She reached out with her wizard-senses, and found the same total nothingness that had permeated reality inside the mist from the moment she had entered it.

"I'm not sure I can even do magic any more, master," she used the term that the wizards of Xalax insisted was due as a title for teachers.

Gem chuckled again. "I am not your master, girl. You are not my slave, nor my servant, nor even my bondsman or squire. You should call me 'Gem', for that is my name. Or you can call me by any other title you like. Once we begin your training, you will certainly wish to call me a variety of things, none of them pleasant or polite, but certainly you have no 'master'. Not you! Not ever!"

Ariel sat up and curled her knees against her chest, turning to face Gem. Her arms wrapped around her knees, she took a posture that was relaxed, and unconsciously defensive. She had never felt the need before, but deep in her mind were the ancient human instincts to cover her belly when faced by a predator.

"I'll call you 'Gem' then. But I still can't feel magic here. Not at all. Will I ever feel it again?"

"What you mean," he answered, "is 'will you ever be a dragon again?' Being a wizard is too new to you for you to care much about it. But a dragon is the very core of your being, and you are about to burst from needing to know that."

He paused.

Ariel burned with frustration and embarrassment! He was right, of course, but it shamed her to admit it. Fear, deep fear, pushed her to avoid asking, lest she get an answer she could not abide.

Gem spoke, and Ariel could hear the core of humor, long suppressed, in his chill voice. "I should answer before you try to bite me with those tiny human teeth! Yes, you will be a dragon again! And your children will be dragons, true-born and true-blooded."

Relief filled Ariel to the brim and flowed over. Muscles she hadn't even realized were tensed, suddenly relaxed. A mass that had been crushing her mind vanished, and a gnawing in her stomach turned to a chill and then washed away.

Then she realized the second half of what he'd said. "Children?" she asked.

"Yes. You had sex and then you visited Kamaia and Sherina in their temple. Any female who does that bears children. Healthy ones."

Ariel had never heard of Sherina before, but it was no surprise that Gem would know the name of Kamaia's sister, even if no other did.

"More precisely," he amplified, "you are still a dragon, always have been, and always will be. You're about to ask why you are stuck in your human shape. Here, in my kingdom, no magic is allowed that is not mine. Your first task, as my new apprentice, is to learn how to overcome that.

"I know that you were always interested in my teaching-gems. Especially that emerald I keep trying to get them to stop ignoring."

Ariel was both surprised and not by the revelation that he was the author of the teaching-stones. His knowledge of that eased her last doubts and her attention shifted fully to his instruction.

His other revelation, that she was pregnant, was easier to deal with. When the time came, she would find a place to lay her eggs where she could leave them in safety. That was the dragon way of things. For now, she would learn to be Gem's apprentice-wizard.

Gem's lecturing continued. Apparently, his promise to teach her to be a wizard meant starting right that very instant.

"The magic that makes an elf or a dragon comes from total certainty. Such complete assurance that reality doubts itself and takes the form the elf or dragon is certain of. Sorcerers are simply the human descendants of dragons, their magic diluted but still of the same nature.

"Wizards, on the other hand, must have total doubt. They must be able to control this, but their first ability is to doubt reality so strongly that it loses its rigid adherence to rules and becomes malleable to imagination instead. The dragon has total certainty of reality and doubt of the rules governing himself, the supreme arrogance of knowing that the dragon is not subject to the rules of mere mortals. The wizard has total doubt of reality and total certainty of self.

"Thus the two are impossible to mix. Except for you. You must achieve both states simultaneously."

From that vague and impossible start, the lecture rapidly progressed into specific laws and rules that Ariel must learn with both absolute certainty and total doubt. She was sure that most people would find what he said somewhat confusing, more than a little self-contradictory, probably even insane. But, for her, it resonated with something deep inside her, and she realized that the core of the lesson was to be certain, not of herself, but of her ability to know *anything* at all, no matter how impossible. She must remain at a balance point on an unattainably thin line between being able to know anything, and being able to doubt anything, at will.

She must not let what she knew dictate what she could know.

It was a strange way of thinking. A form of pure, postulated knowledge, without precursor or evidence or sense or rationality, but also without the insanity of compulsive contradiction.

Gem answered every question at the moment she thought of it. She had no need to speak. To an outside observer, it would have seemed like a completely one-sided lecture. To Ariel, it was more participatory than any conversation she had ever experienced.

When an undead servant arrived with a mix of freshly killed and still-alive animals, and left them for Gem to deal with, Ariel was startled to realize that hours had passed, and alarmed when her stomach growled at her.

Gem gestured at the animals. "Eat now if you like, or I can cook them for you if you prefer."

Ariel asked him to cook the meat for her. Half because she knew it would be easier to eat that way in her human form, and half because she wanted to see him use magic to cook it. She was disappointed when he summoned more servants and had them build a small campfire in his throne-room and then cooked the dead rabbits over the flame on a simple spit.

More hours flew by. Gem teaching, Ariel listening, with barely a question crossing her mind before he was already answering it.

When she was hungry, she ate while she listened.

When she had other bodily needs, she listened while she crouched over a bucket that was whisked away by undead servants as soon as she was done.

When she could stay awake no longer, Gem provided blankets and a makeshift mattress and pillow for her, and watched over her sleep.

Day after day, she listened.

And she learned.

Weeks went by. Only sleep kept her from her incessant lessons.

Gem made her exercise, so her living body would stay healthy, but even the exercise was accompanied by more lessons.

She grew stronger in a mortal sense. Muscles powered by their own strength, instead of dragon-magic, grew within her. Her bones, her tendons and ligaments, her heart and lungs, all grew stronger. The promise that she was still a dragon, and would have the might of her birthright, motivated her, where it could easily have made her question the need for merely physical strength.

Then he began to exercise her will and her mind. The discipline she had learned in her physical exercise, the focus-of-will she had learned in Xalax, were nothing compared to the demands Gem put upon her mind and spirit!

Exercises she thought she had mastered long ago, of imagination and focus, were revisited and she found that her prior instructors had not taken her a tenth of the way down that long road!

Months went by and she grew stronger in body and soul. And she listened.

She was listening when he told her, "You must not ask the Void for power. You must put power there and expect that the Void will obey. Don't demand. Don't request. Don't hope for it. Do not imagine ever that there is any limit that you cannot surpass. The limits don't exist. Only you do. And the power of the Void is not something that answers to your will. It isn't external to you at all! It IS you! You ARE the Void, you ARE the power, you are your own will and desire and imagination. These are not externalities. You do not try to imagine something. You create it and it is!"

A thousand lessons, a million thoughts, connected for her! Light filled Ariel's eyes. It remained there when her eyes were no longer human. Swirling liquid gold in a face of obsidian scales looked down at Gem. He nodded briefly in satisfaction and continued his lesson.

Her senses bloomed! She could see! She could hear! She could sense the patterns all around her!

The mist, omnipresent, was simply Gem's will acting on the world. It no longer precluded her will, because she did not expect it to. She and he could work together to create a mutual existence. He was still immensely stronger than she in the realms of wizardry and magic. Ariel could tell now that he always would be. But she was a dragon! Always had been, always would be.

The lessons only got tougher after she learned to manifest her own magic in his realm.

It should have been easier, since she no longer needed sleep or rest of any sort. Instead, he had her exercising her body and will in ways that no dragon had ever tried before, and she was in constant pain from the exertion.

Months turned into years. Every day, sometimes every hour, she grew stronger and more powerful.

And every year, she found that Gem had been holding back. No matter how strong she became, he was always far, far more powerful than she could ever hope to match. He could always push her beyond any limit that she conceived. With each new accomplishment, each new barrier shattered, he presented her with the next step, the next barrier, the next freedom to struggle towards.

Then, one day, she realized she knew his core secret! She had learned from the so-called-wizards of Xalax that magic came from setting patterns. Each tiniest sliver of time saw the death of the existing universe and the creation of a new one, based on the patterns set by the prior. Motion and change were illusions created by the perceptions of the human mind to account for the gradual replacement of particles in one space by particles in another. Nothing really moved, in the sense that human eyes saw motion, nothing really changed in the way that the human mind thought of it. All magic was taking the new creation and pushing it into patterns that were different than what the prior existence, now gone, would have transformed into on its own.

People saw a wizard call down magefire, and they thought this was POWER. But they didn't realize that the most powerful wizardry took immense amounts of time. Slow, gradual changes to the very nature of reality itself.

Like the fortifications of Xalax. The flying towers were not something that had been made in an instant. They were slowly crafted over time and with the power of dozens of wizards. At first, reality fought back against them and they required constant, titanic effort to keep even one floating above the ground. Slowly, they were accepted. They turned into something that every living person expected, and they became easier and easier to hold, easier and easier to make. Till, one day, after centuries and generations, they were something any wizard could set in motion in just a few years, and could expect it to last even beyond his own death.

But all of this came from the creation of each new instant. Gem had, by means no other wizard had yet discovered, learned to use the power of the death of the prior instant as well as the birth of the new. Using one or the other was much the same. Using both did not merely double his mastery of nature and reality, it magnified it beyond imagining!

Ariel knew that the beating heart of the school at Xalax was the tiny world-shard hidden in the cliffs behind it. Magic was easier in there, and it was a nearly-impregnable fortress as well. She had been led to believe that the Lady Magistrix created it, and that she was the only wizard powerful enough to have done so.

Being in Gem's "Deadlands", she saw how wrong that was. Gem had obviously created that pocket-sized world and hidden it. It was the prototype, the first attempt, and his new kingdom was the culmination. A shard that existed in two worlds at once, with rules in one that were set by Gem's imagination and postulate, and the "real world" masked behind it.

When she had regained her trueform, she hadn't overcome him or his realm. She had, instead, mastered her ability to be in two worlds at once! Play two games at the same time.

On the day she realized this, she flew up and up. With no prompting from Gem, she took her own initiative and flew into the realms beyond the world, where only dragons can safely go. She left behind the element of earth the moment she lifted off from the ground. In minutes she left behind air and water. With an act of will, she left behind fire and outflew the influence of the world's sun.

Deep in the outer dark of the Void, surrounded on all sides by world-shards but not part of any of them, she drank in the power and majesty that is the birthright of every dragon. Only they can travel from world to world on their own power and by their own will alone. Even wizards must take a part of the worlds with them. Even gnomes must carry the elements with them into the Void or die horribly.

In all her past experience, it had taken an enormous effort to join the realm of a world-shard from the depths of the Void. Sometimes years passed while crossing the barrier into a new world's reality.

She looked at the world below her. Her dragon eyes showed her kingdoms and cities on all continents. Despite the rumors in Xalax, there were cities everywhere. And wizards in all of them. Xalax was the biggest, and showed the most influence of wizards and magic, but every one of them was lit from within by the desires and intentions of living people. Patterns were created and shaped by myriad souls, sometimes in harmony, sometimes in conflict. Life everywhere wove the world around it, and no place in the world, not the deepest desert or the most frozen glacier, was exempt.

This must be what worlds look like to the gods, she thought.

Then she dove back down into the world.

The passage took but an instant! Her ability to live in two or more worlds at the same time made the transition timeless.

She watched with interest as a huge thunderstorm was spawned by the interface between her reality and that of the world at large.

A monstrous bolt of lightning flashed across the interface and slammed thunder into her ears and body. But dragons are made to survive such things, even shrug them off, and she paid it no more heed than she paid to the wind and the rain. They were curious things, but of no importance.

She was not surprised to find Gem waiting for her on the roof of his tower. The pouring rain, unprecedented in this desert realm, was no more uncomfortable or inconvenient for his dead body than it was for her draconic one.

"I am ready," she announced simply.

Gem nodded.

Chapter 7: War

Lady Urula, Magistrix of the School at Xalax, was in her bath when she heard the distant mind-voice of one of her old students calling out to her in urgent alarm. Master Rudiju of Loredon was frantic about something and desperately needed to speak to her.

For a few seconds, she considered ignoring him. He had abandoned her hundreds of years ago, and whatever he was afraid of now was hardly her concern. He made his home far from hers, in a mist-shrouded island in the northern seas.

But his mind nattering at hers was a distraction she did not want. Best to speak with him and get it over with quickly!

She allowed him in. In her mind's eye, she could see him, and she knew he could see her. She was nude, beautiful, and half-floating in steaming water. Let him remember what he had given up when he exiled himself from her rule!

The first seconds of contact changed all of that!

He was terrified, hurt, and desperate.

What could possibly threaten a master wizard? What was going on?

"Lady! Lady! We are being attacked! Something terrible came at us out of the mist! It burns our fortresses! It cannot be stopped!"

The Lady jumped out of the bath, magic lifting her clear of the wide, high brim of the tub and drying her instantly. She knew of only one thing in the whole world that could breach the defenses of Loredon.

"Who is it? Who attacks? Is it the ancient threat?" She asked urgently.

"No, Lady! It is something new. Something I have never seen before. Metal giants! Lady! They kill wizards!"

His mental voice rose to even greater heights of panic and terror! "No! They are here! In the fortress! They come for me! I must …." His voice cut off mid-thought, blaring a last burst of horror and pain.

The Lady fell to her knees in shock. He was dead! Something had killed her old student as easily and quickly as a man swats a fly.

In distant Loredon, smoke filled the sky above metal giants that stomped over shattered ruins. Bolts of white-hot light and blasts of lightning flashed from their weapons as they tore through powerful magical defenses and giant blocks of solid rock as easily as a war-dog rips through flesh.

The master wizard and all of his allies were left as piles of smoking ash, as gnomish war machines consumed their souls to power their engines and weapons. Deep in the machines, the unnatural crystals the gnomes used as batteries soaked in the dead souls of wizards and mortals alike, and slaked their violent thirst for power by trapping them forever. Hundreds, even thousands, of trapped souls would channel the power of the Void into the crystals, and gnomish machines fed on that power.

In minutes, they tore down the second most powerful fortress known to the wizards of the world, and left only doom behind.

Such was the power of their most forceful weapons that the earth below them was slain, and its living essence too was absorbed into the powerful crystals that gnomes use as fuel and weapon alike. The desecration of the living world ripped so deep a wound into the fabric of the shard itself that only the world-titan could ever bring life back to those blasted miles.

Still weeping, the Lady called her servants and her advisors to her. A council of the most powerful and ancient master-wizards known to man gathered in her chambers.

Master Salfeld told the Lady, "I have made contact with masters in six of our sister-cities. Two others do not reply and I fear that Thydion and New Armish are dead. I do not know anyone in Chalasea, but my contact in Zintobar tells me that Chalasea has not yet been attacked."

Lady Urula and several others nodded as Salfeld named other wizard-cities. They too had reached out across the miles to old apprentices, friends, even rivals or enemies.

The wizard-cities had no history of friendship with each other. For most of history, they had been at best rivals, and more often than not open enemies. The Lady Magistrix had spent most of her years trying to unite all of the world's wizards under her rule, and all of the wizard-cities beyond Xalax had been founded by rebels against her authority.

It was good to know that only three cities had fallen to the gnomes. It was terrifying to know they had already utterly destroyed three cities before anyone had even known.

The Lady had regained her composure by this time. She looked and sounded regal, strong, and brave as she told them, "We must remain in contact with the other cities. Let old friends know that we will all be better off gathered together. The machines will defeat us separately, or be crushed by our united power!

"Masters! Does any here believe that anything or anyone could stand against all of us, united in our mutual defense? We can shake the foundations of the world, together!

"Old rivalries, old jealousies, ancient quarrels, these must be forgotten in the face of this new threat. Let all know that we welcome everyone, no matter how grievous we once held any transgression, to join us here, at the most ancient center of our power.

"If we have wronged any of them, beg that they put it aside so that we may fight together against this new threat and live to see tomorrow.

"I fear the threat against us is most grave. It is most real and most dire. There must be no fighting, no petty squabbles amongst us. It is time to unite and stand together, for we indeed must all fall if we try to stand apart!"

Everyone cheered.

But not every wizard saw things their way. Dozens refused to bow to the Lady, and tempers flared as ancient feuds reignited. New rhetoric ripped the scabs off of some festering wounds.

As weeks passed, filled with negotiations and arguments, sweet talk and heated words, subtle and outrageous persuasions, it became clear to everyone that the Lady was right. Every living wizard in the world would unite in Xalax. Some would travel there and be part of her mighty army, and the rest would die horribly under assault from tiny men and their giant machines.

For they had learned somewhat of their implacable and deadly foe. At first, the Lady Magistrex was relieved to find it was not her most ancient enemy somehow returned. They were a tiny people who referred to themselves as "gnomes". The metal giants were artificial steeds they had made for themselves. Each of the sixty-foot-tall war machines housed a dozen or more gnomes as drivers, engineers, and gunmen. Their officers had absolute command and power over them.

And they learned that the gnomish machines were powered by the trapped souls of wizards and dragons. Everyone knew that Dragonhome was destroyed, now they learned it was these people who had done it. Hope disappeared as they learned more and more exactly how deadly their enemy was.

How could anything stand against an army that had slain thousands of the most powerful dragons? That had consumed whole worlds of wizards?

Every person they killed gave the gnomes more power. Even the slight spark of plants and lesser animals fueled their mighty war-engines and their unstoppable weapons. A mortal human consumed by their power-gems might fuel a lightning weapon for a few seconds. A wizard was virtually unlimited force, and the gnomes lusted for that power!

The next two cities fell almost without a fight, for nearly every wizard in them had evacuated to Xalax. On magical winds or riding enchanted horses, on flying carpets and ships that sailed without wind and through land as easily as sea, by a dozen means, they fled before the fury of the gnomes.

Some few looked back and watched the gnomes attack. These, who had seen the enemy, spoke with the Lady.

"We are doomed," they said in various ways. "Nothing can stand against them. Archmagus Kildren called up magefire and voidwalls, and the gnomish machines shrugged off the fire and their weapons tore through the walls."

Kildren had been one of the deadliest war-wizards. But the Lady was more powerful than even he, and many looked to her as their salvation. After all, what other option did they have?

***

The gnome army drove north from their latest conquest. A fortified city in a noisome swamp lay in ruin behind them, its wizards and peoples dead and consumed. Their next goal was a small island that their instruments told them held a small number of powerful wizards who lived in a single very large tower.

Gnomish infantry scouts reported a strange storm approaching from the north, from the general area of their target. They saw the sky turn black, but instead of the usual thunder from such a storm, this one made a deep roaring noise, with an annoying subsonic in it. That it approached across the winds was no surprise, for wizards do such things easily. The gnomes had long experience with fighting against wizards, and an unnatural storm was the least of the threats they had faced many times. A thousand wars on a thousand worlds, and the gnomish army had never yet known defeat, or even significant setback.

The storm was approaching fast, and ten-thousand infantry had to suddenly find or build shelter. The gnomes who manned the dozen mechs assigned to this army had, of course, no such need, and merely watched the approaching storm on their instruments. It was barely interesting to them.

The captain of one of the mechs, named Tever, wished he'd been given a better assignment. There was no glory, and would be little enough fuel, in a single tower that appeared to house less than a dozen wizards. It was, of course, better than guard duty, but he was itching to attack the large city on the middle continent of this world. Sensors and probes said there was more wizardry there than anywhere else on this pitiful little world.

Like most gnomes, Tever was a little more than two feet tall, ugly as sin by human standards, with a simian jawline, mottled skin in shades of off-white and mold-green, a nose that bulbed almost four inches out from between his beady eyes, and a mop of grayish hair. He had two or three gnomish girlfriends in every port, and was considered quite the Lothario by his brothers-in-arms.

His immaculate uniform, charcoal gray with black piping, was stylish, neatly pressed, and dressed tastefully with medals for his bravery, his loyalty to the gnome empire, and his perfect attendance at temple events.

He was idly speculating whether he had offended someone who had gotten him assigned to this crappy little assault, or if this was someone's idiotic idea of giving him a well-earned break. That's when the ground under his army erupted at the same moment the "storm" arrived.

Infantry huddled on the ground, prepared for a wizard-driven thunderstorm, such as they had weathered a hundred times before on a dozen worlds, were horrified when it came upon them.

This was no weather!

This was not rain, or wind or storm!

Uncountable red-and-gold wasps descended on the unprepared gnomes! Their numbers darkened the sky and blotted out the sun!

In an orgy of stingers and sharp jaws, they fastened themselves over every inch of skin and each stung and stung and stung again! Tiny razor-sharp mandibles ripped into flesh in a million bites, ravaging eyelids and faces and creeping inside clothing and armor to bite everywhere!

Thousands of helpless gnomes tried desperately to swat and stomp them away! Some flung themselves into fires, immolating themselves in their agony and panic!

Wasps forced their way into nostrils, ears, mouths, and stung and bit and stung again the soft flesh inside!

Few noticed as the ground poured forth an equal army of large red-and-gold ants, armed with acid-tipped stingers and monstrous jaws!

The giant war machines lurched into battle, each blast of their weapons killing thousands, even millions of the deadly insects! But even millions were but a tiny fraction of this enemy!

Wasps and ants flew and crawled into air-vents on some of the giants. Where the vents had been sealed, they chewed through the seals and gaskets of the mechs.

Thousands of wasps and ants died, twitching in poisoned agony, as they ate through air-filters. For every one that died, thousands took its place.

Captain Tever watched in horror as his whole army was eaten alive and as the lights and power went out of mech after mech!

Then he heard a faint buzz from behind him.

Eyes wide, he smashed the first wasp with his hand. A sickening crunch and it was dead. Even dead, it left its stinger in the flesh of his palm!

Two more crawled out of the vent. He slapped at these, too, and at the warrior-ants that joined them and soon he was stomping and slapping at growing swarms.

Every moment, more and more stingers got past his waving arms and flailing feet.

He felt something crawling on his skin inside his pants, and tried to swat it, but it bit deep into his flesh as it died.

Howling in growing agony, he fell to the floor. Dozens of stingers poured acid-venom into his skin. His flesh was flayed by their jaws. One eye was already swollen shut. Raw agony poured through him as one bit the end of his tongue.

The insects abandoned him just short of death and gathered in a writhing, crawling pile on the floor beside him.

His one eye, watering from endless pain, watched in renewed horror as they melted into each other, flowing like melted wax into a terrible caricature of a person.

She took on flesh and features, hair and nails and skin and bones forming before his tortured eye, till she stood above him as a perfect gnomish woman.

She said something to him as he lay there dying. He could not recognize her words, for she and he spoke no language in common. But he needed no translation. "Now you die," was what he heard, and he could only hope she spoke true.

Sam looked down at the creature on the floor. He was dying, and she had killed him. But she would let him suffer for a while first. Her very existence had only the purpose to defend the tower, and she had done that. She could have saved him, but nothing dictated that she had to be nice to these killers. They were mean!

As the last gnome in that army died, the gnomes suffered their first full defeat ever. In a dozen other locations, they marched from victory to victory. In the end, when they killed this world, Sam's victory would mean very little.

***

Lady Urula was looking at a tiny emerald. The knowledge it recorded was forbidden, on pain of death. The only use she allowed for it was determining how strong a wizard might become, and it was only used for that because the school had no other means to assess strength – at least, none that didn't involve a magical duel to the death, which would have defeated the purpose.

She knew that the lore and exercises in that gem would awaken power beyond anything any wizard should even strive for. It corrupted souls and blasted sanity for those few who could even attempt to work with it.

Many times in the thousands of years since it had been gifted to her, she had been tempted to destroy it. Sometimes the only thing that had stopped her was the suspicion that she would be unable to do so. Its creator, after all, was the only wizard she had ever met who was more powerful than she.

It amused her that she was the one who taught him to imprint his thoughts and knowledge into gemstones. That he had taken her little trick and turned it into the single best means of teaching wizards their craft was no great surprise to her. He took everything magic and made it better, stronger, more powerful, more subtle, more clever.

When they had worked together to create the school, when they were allies and lovers instead of bitter enemies, she had jokingly called them "Gem's gems".

But he had gone where she could not follow. After the First Battle of Xalax, he had slowly grown obsessed with death-magic. Once he was the kindest man she had ever met, despite his unparalleled talent for battle and warfare. In the end, his obsession with death and destruction had driven him to a dark place in his soul. The council had all agreed, after he raised his first undead monstrosity, that he must stop his forbidden research.

He refused her, and she could not abide that! Nobody refused her! It started as a quarrel now and again. Over centuries, heated words became their only words. In the end, he betrayed the whole world by breaking the laws of nature, and she had no choice but to turn on him.

The council had agreed with her plan. They were terrified of Gem's new power, his strength. No few suffered the jealousy of the mediocre for the master, the merely gifted for the true genius. Many sided with Lady Urula out of either personal or sexual loyalty. A few disagreed, and had to be silenced lest they betray, intentionally or not, the plans the council took on.

First, his lady poisoned him. While dragons and elves are virtually immune to most poisons, wizard magic focuses on the external world, and most would have died horribly in a few seconds.

When the poison slowed him down but left him alive, they tried magic. A dozen of the most powerful wizards in the world, and he matched them power for power, spell for spell, and they gained nothing in the fight. Years later, some even speculated that he held back from hurting them, but they never stated such out loud, for speaking of him was forbidden on punishment of death.

When magic didn't work, they resorted to knives, bludgeons, even throwing things. A few grappled with him. He was, by far, the more skilled warrior, but numbers eventually won. Two of the council lay dead, three more would need the help of

Kamaia's temple to ever walk again, but Gem lay dead at their feet, bled out and mangled horribly.

He stood up from that, powered by unholy magic, filled with dark power, and raged at them for their betrayal. Like an angry adult facing rebellious children, he shamed them and called them cowards and worse. Vowing to never again help or heed them, to never again show them any slightest compassion or mercy, he stormed from the city and disappeared into the night.

The lady made all of the council bind themselves with magical oaths to never reveal any of this to anyone. No one would ever speak of Gem again. All histories, all records, all journals that mentioned him would be burned, rewritten, expunged.

Some few outside the council believed Gem was driven off or killed, and his undead monstrosities destroyed with him. Even that belief was discouraged, and soon only those wizards who had known him personally even believed he had ever existed.

She had joined with the council and driven him from Xalax.

The night that the wizards of the world gathered in Xalax to plan their last defense of their own lives and the world they lived in, doubts haunted the Lady Magistrix of Xalax. Vanity and pride kept her sure that he could not help, would not help, had indeed never been needed and was not yet.

Even so ... If he was still out there somewhere. If he was – not alive, but not truly dead – even yet. If. If. If.

She set the gem down forcefully. The lore in there would not help her. Even if it were possible to master it in the weeks they had left before the gnomes attacked Xalax, she would rather be destroyed than violate her passionate belief that he was wrong and she was right. That she was still righteously angry, and that he could never, in all the time of immortal wizards, ever reconcile himself with her. That he could ever be forgiven for his ancient transgressions against her.

* * *

The whole gnomish army was gathered south of the huge mountains that split the world in two. It was poised to cross the passes, crushing all opposition, and assault the last stronghold of wizardry in the whole world.

The other cities, schools, even hermits, had been hunted, assailed, destroyed, or driven here.

It would take a few days to cross the mountains.

Xalax knew they were coming, and the city prepared for war.

A stream of civilians fled to the north, the west, even east into the high plateaus. The streets were empty of any who did not intend to fight.

A few, hearing the gnomes were finally entering the passes and starting the battle, regretted their decision to stay and wished they had left with friends, family, neighbors. But it was far too late for that.

Lieutenant Charther, in his flying tower above the pass, died fighting. It was futile, and all who stayed with him knew it, but they would not abandon their post. Many brave men died in a single blast from a mech's hell-weapons.

Only one of the tower guards who, years ago, had lusted after Ariel on her first arrival in their world, lived long enough to see the gnomes with is own eyes. It would have been a mercy if he had died of frozen wind and snow. The gnomes found him barely alive, and quickly hooked him into their machines, where his body was reduced to fine ash and his soul was consumed to power their crystalline hell.

For the second time in its long history, Xalax prepared for overwhelming war.

This time, they had no half-finished log palisade, guarded by street-thugs hurriedly supplied with quasi uniforms and tools appropriated as makeshift weapons.

This time, they had vast walls of enchanted stone and wizard-wrought steel. Their gates were thick and strong. Their guards were professional soldiers, war-hardened trolls, veteran battle-mages, armed with enchanted weapons and dressed in magical armor.

On the walls and the high cliff behind the city were their most powerful and impressive guardians. Hundreds of master-wizards, thousands of journeymen and apprentices.

Deep in the city, in their temple, Kamaia and her sister prepared their priests and priestesses to heal those injured in battle. The favorite daughters of the world-titan would stand as his last line of defense if they had to. When they had to. Until they could not.

All prepared for one last battle. All else had been lost, there was nowhere to flee that the gnomes would not follow.

And all knew, in the end, this massive preparation for defense would avail them nothing. The city had just as little hope as the last time. But this time, there was no wizard-mercenary coming to save them. This time, even the Lady had no clever plan to pull them out of the fire.

***

Thousands of miles away, Gem and Ariel were arguing again.

"We must fight!" she yelled. She was wearing her human form, beautiful and strong. Her eyes flared and wizard-power wreathed her in her passion.

"Why?" he demanded. His raspy voice carried no emotion of its own, but his aura was palpable to everyone in the room, living or dead. "They hate me. They exiled me because of their own fear. They would rather die and be consumed by the gnomes for their war-engines than be helped by me!"

They had fought over this many times. Truces barely held between fights, while Ariel continued her studies and practices and Gem cared for his slowly growing kingdom. This time, Ariel knew she would have to convince him or she would never win. She had known that exact same thing the last five times they had fought over it.

She had tried appealing to his love of people, to no avail.

She had attempted to argue that the death of the world would destroy his kingdom. But they both knew that was untrue even before she started.

She once even argued that there would be no more dead to recruit to his fortress and lands if the world died. She was right, but he did not seem to care.

There was no point arguing that the gnomes would attack him next. He knew that, and knew how dangerous they were, and merely replied, "Then we will fight."

Sometimes, she wondered if his obsession with death had finally defeated him, and he was actually hoping to die under assault from gnomish weapons. Nothing else could kill him, and he had no more horizons to explore, no more mysteries to solve. Maybe he hoped for actual death. But that argument was pointless. If right, it would not help. If wrong, it would only harm her cause.

This time, she argued her deepest truth.

"Because they killed my father and I want them dead!" she yelled. "And I will fight them alone if you will not!" She was horrified by the words that had just come out of her mouth, because she knew they were true, and she knew she would die and be consumed by the soul-gems if she fought alone. And she knew that would not stop her.

"Fight for me, if not for yourself, or anyone else. Please," she begged.

***

The wizards of Xalax stretched forth their power, and brought the stone and ice of the mountains crashing down on the gnomes. Passes disappeared as the land twisted and tore itself from deep within.

The force of their opening attack shook the ground for hundreds of miles in all directions.

The gnomes had come prepared for that. Mechs burned and blasted their way out from under thousands of tons of rock and ice. A few infantry died, crushed by the world they were invading, but not enough to matter.

Most of the flying towers were abandoned, as they had no purpose against this invader. But a few hid wizards brave enough to give their lives for a chance to strike the gnomes while they were still miles away from the city.

As soon as the giant mechs came into sight, these few fools conjured magefire, or clouds of poison gas, or bolts of lightning, each as his skill and personality inclined him.

Thousands of gnome soldiers were burned, vaporized, poisoned, even frozen, by the wizards. But thousands more held up shields that resisted magical force and were protected from the spells.

And the mechs never felt a thing.

The gnomes counter-attacked, and wizards died screaming as their living essence was torn apart and fed into the soul-gems. Mech after mech gained power from each wizard it consumed. In a few minutes, the vanguard of the wizards' defense would be turned against the very thing they tried to defend, their souls used as fuel for the attack on their home.

In the early morning light, before the sun had crested the eastern cliffs, the gnomes approached their final destination in this world.

The next line of defense was an army of battle-mages and trolls. Tens-of-thousands of immortal soldiers and almost unkillable monsters ambushed the gnomes and tore into their ranks.

A wave of steel and claws ripped thousands of gnomes to shreds in seconds!

The mechs didn't pause. This was not their fight, nor their objective. They marched on, impervious to the soldiers around them. Where they stepped, they left the crushed remains of soldiers from both armies, with no care for the mixed pools of blood.

There were sixty of them, all of the mechs in the world, and they were not even slowed by the mightiest army the wizard-cities had ever assembled.

Ahead of them, the forbidding stone walls of Xalax loomed. Towers and battlements, reinforced gates and the innumerable and exotic weapons the wizards themselves would wield.

Beams of light so hot that steel turned to flaming vapor on its touch flashed from the mechs and ripped the walls to rubble.

Bolts of lightning blasted from them, shattering everything in their path! The world shuddered at the artificial thunder. Strong-walled homes crumbled from the unnatural torture of the very air itself!

Mighty fortifications that had withstood every assault for thousands of years were torn away before the sun had finished rising.

The Lady looked out over the battle from her perch high on the cliffs. She knew that she would have to retreat into the school soon, but she had hoped, vainly, that the city would stand a little longer than it had.

All her life had been in this city.

And now, before her eyes, it was destroyed.

In the city's tortured body, between the walls of the school and the rubble that was the only remains of the outer fortifications, all that still stood was the sisters' temple. She was not surprised that it withstood, for a time, the hell-attack of the gnomish machines. She respected the power of the sisters and their father, the world-titan. In all the city, only they were mightier than she.

The rest of the city was smoking ruin, and the mechs were advancing across it.

She was surprised, however, that all of them were converging on the temple. It appeared that she and the school might outlive the sisters after all. Even if only for a few minutes.

All of the city's defenses had been spent. Thousands of wizards dead, and, so far as the Lady could see, they had destroyed only one mech. It stood, smoke pouring out of every aperture, where a dozen wizards and hundreds of trolls had assaulted it. The warriors and wizards who had attacked the mech died to the last man, but they had managed, through combination of luck, skill and courage, to strike down at least one of the monstrous machines.

***

The mech captains gathered their machines around the temple. This was their main goal. The wizards left in the cliff-fortress a short distance away were just fuel, and could wait. Killing this place, where the world-titan communed with his creation, was their main objective.

This would kill the world itself! Their god's commandment, to slay all worlds that were not perfect, would be fulfilled!

For, of course, only the gnomes were perfect. Their leaders told them so. And all that was not perfect must be destroyed, to clear the way for a universal perfection that could only come when all flawed worlds, beings, peoples, had been removed and nothing remained but perfection itself.

Thus they were commanded. And thus they obeyed.

The mechs aimed their terrible weapons at the temple, and waited. The titan would defend this place. And he would die. And his world would die with him.

***

The Lady and six of her most powerful councilors watched from their balcony on the cliff. They weren't sure what the gnomes were doing, but they felt that it would be soon.

A few prayed.

Most were too overwhelmed to have even that much hope.

And then SOMETHING rose up from the temple! Awesome in might and majesty, a presence that radiated PATTERN and INTENTION in ways no wizard could ever hope to emulate, poured into the stone and the air and the filled the ruined city with POWER!

The Lady and her people watched in helpless horror as all of the gnomish machines fired at the presence in unison.

The beams they had used on walls and towers, wizards and soldiers and trolls, were candles in the sun compared to the might they poured into this!

Every human mind still alive in all the world reeled as a scream of anguish and horror poured from the temple!

Lady Urula and her people were the only witnesses as Kamaia leapt into the beams intended for her father!

No one even noticed when the city was plunged into darkness by a sudden storm-cloud that boiled into the sky above it. Their doom was upon them, and a strange storm had no importance. Perhaps it was even poetic, in its dark way.

A dozen miles away, gnomes were locked in battle with trolls and battle-mages. When Kamaia screamed, every troll in the army went berserk! Raging hunger and pain ripped into them and drove them insane! Gentlemanly Gregory, honorable and steadfast, grappled the soldier nearest him and bit his head off! Eyes wild with feral rage, he bit chunks off of everything he could grab and ate and ate and ate, heedless of the blood, the pain, the shock and terror that spread around him and every other troll!

***

The gnome captain was surprised when one of the lesser spirits of the temple blocked the beams for a moment. That one must have been immensely powerful, almost a world-titan herself, to stop these weapons for even a moment!

He snarled as the world-titan, wounded and torn but still alive, retreated deep into the shard. Damn that lesser spirit! Now they would have to work for it! The titan wouldn't be stupid enough to rise again, and they would have to dig deep and hard to chase it down and slay it! Their plans would be delayed by years because of her!

It would only take a few minutes to charge up the guns again, but those guns were useless without the right kind of target.

He did not pay attention when the sunlight outside his mech was suddenly cut off by a roiling mass of clouds.

He barely noticed when lightning began raining down all around, but dismissed it as a last-ditch attempt by the wizards to save themselves.

Didn't they know that lightning couldn't hurt the mechs? And this lightning wasn't even striking them!

***

Something was moving on the ground around the mechs.

The Lady was the first to see it.

It was dark, and something was obscuring her wizard-vision, so she couldn't quite tell what horror the gnomes were unleashing down there.

Lightning was striking the ground all around the war machines, and each bolt left behind … something.

Magic shielded her eyes from the worst of the flare, or she would have already been blinded by the blaze of the gnome-weapons.

The thunder of a thousand bolts of lightning was mere noise compared to the blastings of the mechs!

***

A gnome captain, secure in the command center of his giant mech, noticed that there was a strange smell in the air. He looked around and saw that mist was forming in his command center. That was certainly unusual!

They were waiting for weapons to be ready again. Hoping the titan would return. It was worth a few minutes delay if it gave them a second chance at that target. He knew it was a mostly forlorn hope, but they had nothing else to do till engineers could dig the tunnel to the titan's core, so waiting seemed appropriate.

Frustrated, bored and mildly curious, he gestured to one of the engineers and pointed at the mist. "Is there something wrong with the air systems?" he asked.

The engineer frowned. He was about to reply that he would check, when something stopped his voice in his throat.

There were eyes in the mist!

Two eyes burned at him from inside the growing cloud! They locked gazes with him, and terror filled every fiber of his being!

The captain, perplexed, watched his engineer stare into the mist. What was wrong with the man? He was pale as a sheet of paper and frozen where he stood!

A tendril of faintness stretched out from the still-growing main body of mist. It fumbled towards the engineer, and then reached into his gaping mouth.

The gnome captain could not believe what he was seeing! Mist doesn't do that!

Blood fountained from the engineer's mouth! A stream of sickening crimson poured through the air, through the tendril, into the mist!

All five gnomes on the command deck stared in abject horror, frozen where they stood or sat, as something solidified out of the blood and mist.

Their limbs were paralyzed as its voice filled their minds and its eyes filled their locked gazes.

"So tasty," whispered the vampire's mental voice from the congealing mist. "So tasty! And the master says we must eat them all! The master is so kind! We love the master!"

***

Inside the fortified center of another mech, a gnome watched all the lightning pouring down around him. One of the flashes was so close that it threw an ink-dark shadow on the front wall of his small chamber.

After a moment, he remembered that was impossible. He wasn't looking through windows, he was watching through instruments that were purpose-made to filter out over-bright flashes. So how was there a shadow on the bulkhead ahead of him?

It wasn't his shadow. Most of the light came from the instruments in front of him. If he cast a shadow, he reasoned, it would be behind him. Perplexingly, this was in front of him. He glanced over his shoulder, and there was no source of light behind him. But the shadow in front of him, cast on the instrument panel, persisted! How strange!

And it didn't quite look like his shadow anyway. Something was off about the shape or … no … the movements. It moved even when he didn't, and its arms were still even though his were moving.

In all his decades of battling wizards and every variety of threat from a dozen worlds, he had never seen anything like this.

Fascinated and morbidly curious, he couldn't ignore the strange thing.

He reached out his finger to touch it.

He was alone in a sealed room, contained by heavy blast-proof doors, so nobody heard his scream.

His body, drained and mummified, aged a hundred years in a second, would never be found.

The shadow slipped across the room and faded through the back wall. There were more of them in the next room, and the master had asked it, so nicely, so politely, to consume them all.

When it passed over one of the soul-gems embedded in the back wall, the gem faded and cracked, then crumbled to dust. The scraps of souls and the dregs of life trapped in the crystal fed the shadow-wraith a feast. But even that wasn't enough for the undead darkness' infinite hunger. It hunted on.

***

Two mech-crews, enraged by the traitors around them, fought to the death! Bolts of energy blasted from mech to mech! Shields of pure force deflected the power, but at a cost.

It would take them several minutes to drain each other's crystals of all power. The gnomes, trapped inside powerless mechs, would turn to fighting each other.

Gem knew exactly how it would end.

He knew how long it would take.

But it was okay, he had time.

***

Ariel finished her storm. She had carried every undead she could with her to the battlefield.

Now it was time to fight!

She knew that breathing dragonfire on a gnome mech was useless. They were manufactured to withstand exactly that.

But she could move in and out of realms and shards now.

She was curious what would happen if she blew dragonfire inside a mech?

It turned out that she kind of liked the smell of burning gnomes.

Appendix

People	Notes
Gem	Arch-wizard. Human male. Black skin, sapphire-blue eyes.
Ariel	Dragon female. The only survivor of the gnome attack on Dragonhome. The only dragon-wizard in all the worlds.
Lady Urula/Magistrix	Human noblewoman and wizard. Rules the city of Xalax.
Gregory	Troll. A soldier of Xalax and friend of Ariel.
Sam	Hive-mind insectiform polymorph. Not a wizard, but spent enough time around them that she can help teach apprentices. Appears in "Story", "Second Story", and "Third Story". Older than the world, and nobody (but maybe the gods) knows where she comes from.

Places	
Dragonhome	A tiny world-shard that only dragons could get to, till the gnome wars. Destroyed early in the gnome wars.
Xalax	Ancient city founded by nonborn. Home to the leading wizard school of the world-shard.

Terms	
Battle-Mage	Human warriors granted extraordinary power by the wizards of Xalax.
Dragon	A race of humans who used immensely powerful magic, with the help of world-titans, to transform themselves into semi-reptilian demigods that can survive on any world and can travel the void between worlds. Most can assume a human form that corresponds to who they would be without magic. Some can take multiple humanoid forms. All are immensely powerful, effectively immortal, and very dangerous.
Elf	A race of humans who use internally

	directed magic to "perfect" themselves and achieve a form of limited immortality.
Troll	Human warriors transformed by the wizards of Xalax into war-machines. Average 10' tall (3m), with claws, fangs, armored skin, and the ability to recover from wounds almost instantly. Effectively immortal unless killed by magic, or burned to ash. Before the gnome wars, they were known for their honor, bravery, and devotion to the temple of Kamaia, who helped the wizards create them. Driven insane in the gnome wars.
Void	The space between worlds. Perceived by humans as the space between worlds and stars. Perceived by wizards as a chaos of power and creative potential. Perceived by dragons as a vortex of energy that can be flown through by adult dragons. Deadly to anyone except dragons exposed to it in its raw form.
Wizard	Any living creature that can use the creative power of the void between worlds to corrupt, override, or manipulate the rules of the world-shards. Most start out human. There are no elf-wizards or dragon-wizards (one exception).
World-Shard	A partially or fully formed world placed in the void by the gods during the creation of all reality. Look like planets or stars to humans. Look like "islands in the sky" to wizards and dragons. They have different elements and different rules, but humans can only experience the rules of their own birth-world, so perceive them as variations from their own world. Only wizards and dragons can see worlds as they truly exist in the Void.
World-Titan	Worlds are made of spirits. Wind, Earth, Fire, Water, Life, and sub-forms (examples:

Fox spirits, Storm spirits, Wave spirits). The most powerful of these spirits are the world-titans, who are the incarnations of the power that makes whole worlds. These spirits have the potential to become totems for people, usually human, who then gain some degree of the essence and power of the spirit.

Notes on Ariel's journey:

The geography is "based on a real world" in the Hollywood sense of "it's mostly made up, but there are semblances to something you might recognize".

Assume the base-geography is Earth in the physical spaces and arrangements. There's a large continent that corresponds physically to Eurasia, and another for Africa, and again for the Americas. There are oceans strongly resembling those of Earth. The details are frequently different, but the overall shape and terrain would be familiar.

Given that, and with the understanding that these places don't match in culture, history, or any other particulars:

- Xalax is north of the Himalayan mountains, near a plateau sort of like Tibet.
- Ariel arrives in the world in a mountain pass that would be in Afghanistan on Earth.
- The Place of Angels is so obviously Los Angeles I feel embarrassed writing this note.
- Gem's undead citadel is in the general area of the Mojave Desert. A place that might be called "Death Valley" is nearby...
- Sam's tower is an obvious rip-off of the Empire State Building and corresponds to it in most particulars.
- The rest can be extrapolated by looking at a globe and tracking between these points.